PASSION PATROL SERIES
WEALTH

Hot Cops. Hot Crime. Hot Romance.

By
Emma Calin

WEALTH

FIRST PUBLISHED 2019
BY GALLO-ROMANO MEDIA
COPYRIGHT © 2019 EMMA CALIN
ISBN 13: 9781916097506

Table of Contents

Wealth   1

A Message from Emma   189

A FREE Book for you   190

More books by Emma Calin   191

About Emma Calin   208

Find Emma Online   209

Publisher   210

WEALTH

By Emma Calin

Chapter 1

"Oscar-Lima-Three to Oscar-Control, we've got a lot of Italian sports car French kissing an English oak tree. Looks like only bent metal. Standby for update. Over."

Police Constable Kaitlyn Thorn re-clipped her shoulder radio mic, killed the siren of her BMW 530d patrol car as she updated traffic control at Scotland Yard. She stepped out and assessed the scene with quick eyes that had seen it all before; well maybe not quite all. This was an odd one. Straight dry tarmac, 2 p.m. on a fine autumn day in a quiet South London suburban street. A Maserati GranTurismo cabriolet in collision with a tree. Low speed impact. A guy was standing by the vehicle making a call on his cellphone. She let him talk, noting his size, age, and spectacular condition. Blood was trickling from his temple, dripping from his chin onto the lapel of his expensive gray business suit. He was alive and clearly fit.

She checked the interior for casualties, pushing away the deployed airbag. A Gucci briefcase was open on the front passenger seat. A neat folder was embossed with the vulture and bankroll crest of Sackman-Platinum Bank. Something out of place caught her eye. She reached out to recover it.

"You'll need a warrant," said a deep voice as a large hand gripped her forearm.

"You'll need to know how to get out of handcuffs if you don't let go," she said, half turning to stare hard into the tanned, handsome face of the guy she assumed was the driver.

He released his hold and stood back, leaving his calm brown eyes on hers. Like this banker type could just touch a cop and make eyes at her. She pulled her gaze away and reached back into the briefcase to retrieve the item that had caught her attention.

"What's this?"

"You're the police officer," he said.

She rolled a heavy caliber lead shotgun pellet between her fingers.

"Maybe we'll save the difficult questions for an interview at the station. Are you the driver?"

"What interview at the station?"

"Last time I'm going to ask you. Are you the driver?"

"Ah huh."

"Have you been drinking?"

"Nope."

"Drugs?"

"Caffeine."

"I require you to provide a specimen of breath. Come with me to the police car."

"I told you, I haven't been drinking."

"I require you to provide a specimen of breath for analysis," she said.

He shrugged and studied the number on her uniform epaulets. "It's your time to waste, constable eight-three-eight."

"Blow into this...."

She checked the intoximeter. Negative.

"So what happened?" she asked.

"Can't remember."

"Did you black out? Be careful how you answer. If you tell me you lost consciousness before the crash you're going to lose your license."

She held his eyes.

"Are you trying to be kind to me?"

"You've heard of good cop bad cop? We're short of staff so I cover both jobs."

She could never resist playing life for the jokes. He was smiling, then laughing all the way to his dark eyes.

"At least you can still see the funny side. Tell me what happened," she said.

"Look, I must have just lost concentration for a second. I think I was checking the fuel gauge or something like that."

This guy was beginning to piss her off. It was a small crash with no major injury. She could wrap it up now, take all his details, call in a damage only, no allegations, a classic NFPA—no further police action. She could. She was off duty in another half hour and she had a karate class.

"I'm going to check out your car and I don't need a warrant."

He walked with her, back to the wreck. He was tall and held himself well. His hair was dark brown, expensively overlong, his nose straight but broad.

"How did you cut your temple?"

"Must have been some glass," he replied.

She had stopped at the driver's door. Shattered glass covered the seat and the floor well. The impact had been to the front.

The impact had been to the front!

Something had smashed the side window. Something like a pellet from a shotgun. The metal of the door was pitted with small dents. A picture formed in her mind. Either way this guy was in trouble. And he was not going to walk away without telling her the truth.

"Just tell me what happened. Don't tell me the tree jumped out or that a guy was shooting rabbits and you got in the way."

He raised his hands in mock surrender.

"I like the rabbit angle. Those huntin' shootin' fishin' types are real mean."

She let out a sigh. Someone had just tried to kill this guy and here he was shrugging it off and giving her that smile. She took her time pulling out her notebook from her hip pocket.

"Name?"

"Randolph Quinn."

"Date of birth?

"24th November, 1988."

"Who owns the car?"

"Me. One of my companies, not sure which one."

"Give me a clue."

"The Church of Mammon."

"Mister, are you just taking the piss or what?"

"As if...."

She called in a car check.

"Oscar-Control to Oscar-Lima-Three. Platinum Maserati GranTurismo. Registered owner Artemis Financial Associates, Canary Wharf. Registered brand new yesterday. No trace lost or stolen."

She called in his personal details. Not known to police. Now she had to make a decision. As far as she could see she had no reason to lock him up. Except maybe to save his life.

He was calmly examining the damage to the car, taking pictures with his cellphone.

"Smile," he said as he focused on her.

"Not part of the service," she snapped back.

"OK. One with your police hat off then—please."

"You're a cocky bastard."

"Just one shot without the hat.

This was stupid and ridiculous. Even with the blood now dried on his face he was gorgeous. He'd adopted an expression of a disappointed boy, his dark eyes turned to a sorrowful pleading. In an impulse she snatched off her white-topped Traffic Patrol cap.

"There!"

"Spiky streaky blond. You've got a special look."

He was beaming a smile and she just couldn't stop that flicker of a response on her lips and deep inside her. She was snapping out of this right now.

"I'm arresting you on suspicion of theft of a motor vehicle. You do not have to say anything but anything—"

"I've seen all that stuff on TV. You've got no grounds to lock me up."

"You didn't know the owner of the car. That's enough suspicion for me. Handcuffs or not?"

He made a show of rubbing his chin in thought.

"On balance, not."

"Mr Quinn, I'm not an idiot. Someone has fired a shotgun at your vehicle causing you to lose control and hit a tree. My guess is that you're the target of a carefully planned hit. Maybe it was a warning, maybe you just got lucky. Maybe the boys are round the corner reloading ready for another go. Maybe I just want to keep you alive for a bit longer. Walking away is just not an option for a cop."

He nodded, his face now serious.

"I do need to get out of here and you know, you're the sort of girl who could take me anywhere."

He collected his briefcase and slumped into the front passenger seat of the police BMW.

"Prisoners go in the back."

"I'm the type of man who sits in the front. I'm quite happy to drive if you need a break. We could be a team."

4

She stared at him. He was so bloody confident and arrogant. Many people would be a trembling wreck in his situation. He was a year older than her but their worlds must be light years apart.

"Where were you brought up?" she asked.

"Croydon—New Addington Estate," he replied in a sudden South London accent. "Poor boy made good—that's me."

She turned her blue eyes to examine his face.

"Just sit there quiet and shut up. We're going in to Brixton police station. You need to talk to the C.I.D."

"I'll only talk to you, OK. I'll tell you my story. We can take it from there."

She knew that would be impossible but she left him in ignorance while she called in to Scotland Yard for a vehicle recovery and a scenes of crime examination. She had to keep professional even though this guy was giving her some twitches she thought had stopped in her teens. She started the motor and responded abruptly.

"Seat belt."

He snapped in as she checked the mirror. A black motorcycle was on the corner of the junction 500 yards behind the police car. Some primitive cop instinct gave her a shiver. She glanced at her passenger. He was flicking through the photos on his cellphone, smiling at the shots he'd taken of her. She glanced back at the mirror. The bike was still there. Two riders in helmets. She was facing away from them, and they wouldn't expect her to come their way. She checked the tension on the handbrake, selected Drive and floored the gas pedal. The tires squealed and smoked as she went full lock and grabbed the brake to spin the car the opposite way. She hit the gas as the BMW straightened up. The bike riders had begun to react. In their place she would have come straight toward her but they weren't trained pursuit drivers. They turned and fled but she'd gotten close enough to read the license plate.

"Be careful—those guys...," he began.

"I told you to shut the fuck up. Now shut the fuck up."

She punched the mic button to transmit live. "Oscar-Lima-Three to Oscar-Control. In pursuit of black motorcycle, north on A23, high speed, approaching traffic lights at South Circular Road. It's a left, left, left toward Clapham."

5

She hit the switches for sirens and blue lamps, swerving through a red light and forcing an extra lane through the traffic. The bike was pulling away, weaving through cars and using the sidewalk. It was still in sight as it hurtled onto the open green of Clapham Common.

"Oscar-Lima-Three to Oscar-Control—they've returned to nature across the grass."

"Roger that. We have them on CCTV. Stand down Oscar-Lima-Three.

She took a deep breath and slapped the steering wheel.

"Sod it. I wanted my hands on those bastards."

"You're not just a pretty face. That was some bit of driving," he said.

"You should see me at the start of my shift and I'm not trying to be any kind of pretty face."

"That's the thing with real pretty girls; they don't have to try. It's just the way they are. I prefer you without the hat. I'd need to make an assessment without the uniform for my final judgment."

She shook her head, outwardly ignoring him, and listened to the police radio. The police chopper India-Nine-Nine had located one of the riders hiding behind a shed in the backyard of a house backing onto the common. He was about to meet a German shepherd police dog.

"Those guys on the bike fired at you didn't they?"

"What kind of young people is our society creating, officer?"

"Cops, bankers, crooks," she said.

He nodded.

"Takes a better man than me to tell the difference."

Chapter 2

The custody sergeant had the slow droop of a long-retired bloodhound. He looked up from the pile of paperwork on his desk.

"What have you got for me young lady?"

"She's got me. It's an unlawful arrest but she means well. Don't be cross with her, inspector. You know how women can be."

"Hmm … clever dick, eh. I'm not an inspector."

"You should be. I'll speak to the commissioner."

The sergeant turned to a young officer who had walked in.

"Martin, search him and put him straight in a cell. I'm not in the mood for comedians."

"Sarge, he's just got too much yap for his own good. He doesn't know who owns the car he's just crashed," said Kaitlyn.

"And someone loosed off a twelve bore to assist his driving skills," added the sergeant.

"My fame always goes ahead of me," said Randolph Quinn.

The sergeant sighed, clearly aware of the story so far.

"Between you and me, son, I can see straightaway why someone would take you out. If I were you I'd be a bit concerned about walking down the steps out of this place. Search him, Martin."

"Can't Miss 838 do it?"

The sergeant ignored his remark and began listing the property.

"Leather Gucci wallet containing cash to value of eight hundred and seventy-one pounds. Chopard Mille Miglia watch. Visa Infinite credit card. Merrill Accolades American Express card, Sackman-Platinum Wings of Wealth card."

"I'll need one of those cards back. I'll have to pop in somewhere to get a new car on the way home," said Randolph.

The custody sergeant turned the Visa Infinite card over in his hand. He looked hard in the face of his prisoner, a faint smile on his lips.

"Infinite wealth?" he asked.

"A fair assessment, I suppose."

"Shame the card isn't in your name," he said.

"Randolph Quinn is my business name."

Kaitlyn caught his eye. He gave her a small lift of his eyebrow.

"So what is your name?"

"Lee Smith, billionaire, at your service," he said.

"So who is Randolph Quinn?"

"He's the true soul of Lee Smith, like the statue hidden inside the stone waiting for the hand of the sculptor."

"You're just so full of shit," she said.

"Sarge, did you hear that? This is police brutality. I'm a victim of crime remember."

"We don't know who you are, you don't know who owns that car, you've got a Mickey Mouse credit card, and somehow you're involved with a firearms incident. You might be with us for a while. You're entitled to a lawyer and to notify someone that you're here. We'll call a police surgeon to look at that cut. Do you have any requests?"

"A nice strong cup of tea with plenty of sugar."

The sergeant nodded.

"Put him in a cell, Kaitlyn. We'll see about the tea."

She banged the door shut and took a final look at him through the grille. The cell block had an odor of vomit, urine, bleach, and man-sweat. She didn't feel proud to leave him here but what the hell? She didn't expect to see him again anyway. She'd give her report to the detectives and she might just catch the last few minutes of her karate class. She watched him sit on the concrete ledge seat that would double as his bed if they kept him in. Just who had fired at him and why? He looked up at the bars and smiled.

"Don't forget the sugar darlin'."

She found herself smiling almost laughing. He had the cheek of Old Nick.

"I'm off duty now," she said.

"I'd get you a cup of tea any time if you hadn't banged me up in jail."

She went to the small utility kitchen and made a cup of tea in a Styrofoam cup, adding two spoons of sugar. She pulled down the grille flap and handed it in to him.

"Thank you, and I mean that, Kaitlyn."

His eyes were still and fixed on her face. She liked him to look at her, liked him to say her name. He was a streetwise London boy from her own place in life.

"You seem more like a Randolph Quinn than a Lee Smith," she said.

"Depends who I'm dealing with. I'd always be your Randolph," he said, gulping at the tea. "Tell your bosses I'll only talk to you. I'll tell them the same. What's not to like?"

"Detectives do what they do. I'm a traffic cop."

"You're one hell of a cop. I'm not saying you've got balls because that would be impolite and as yet I've no personal insights...."

"And you might get a smack in your smooth-tongued gob."

"Lovely tea. Only a real woman could make tea like this."

She looked at his perfect teeth, smiling with full sensual lips that just pushed a slight sense of a kiss into her mind. He was looking back at her lips and she could almost begin to soften her own expression to signal a complicity—or a desire.

"Before I go, I do want to know something. When we were at the car did you know those guys were on that corner with the bike?"

"Yeah, I knew. For a minute I thought you weren't going to arrest me. Then I would have been in the shit. I wasn't exactly expecting the Nascar driving stunt."

"They could have killed both of us."

"I did think of that."

"And...."

"Well, I thought of that because I'm the sort of infallible man who thinks of everything. Mainly I thought they wouldn't want to get involved with cops. I was like that myself before I met you."

"You're a complete bloody con-artist, Lee Smith. Enjoy your tea," she said as she flipped the grille shut. Now she had to begin the writing.

Chapter 3

Although she'd missed the class, Kaitlyn slid her Nissan 350Z Roadster into the car park of the Battersea Sports Centre. Normally she knew how she felt and exactly what she wanted to achieve. This night was just a little bit different. Something had gotten under her skin and she had a name for it, or maybe two. Tonight she needed to share because suddenly a small forgotten light in her had switched on and then gone out. The cruelest thing in a prisoner's cell is a little ray of teasing light. And she'd just slammed it shut. She needed a friend and maybe a drink. And tonight she had something to show off.

"Don't tell me, let me think. Crisis traffic jam in Whitehall and you just couldn't get away."

Kaitlyn hugged her best mate Camille as she came out of the doors.

"Traffic cops don't just do that stuff. What did you detect today on the vice squad? People having sex?"

"Powerless emaciated little cows getting raped for money as it happens," replied Camille with an edge in her voice.

"All I had was a car chase with armed killers and a brush with a billionaire hunk banker who gave me the eye."

"So what are you doing here with me? Why aren't you exposing your show-stopping female allure to his golden gaze?"

"Because I've locked him up in a cell in Brixton nick."

"Romantic or what? What's the charge?"

"Good question. Some thugs loosed off a shotgun at him. He's got couple of different identities and he's vague about who owns his brand new Maserati."

"He's got to be a villain mixed up in some kind of turf war," said Camille with a dismissive wave of her hands.

Kaitlyn stood back from her friend. Camille was a couple of years older, a detective at West End Central for the past five years. She was wiser than the hardest of mean streets. She'd known her since the first day at Hendon Training School. Even then she'd been tougher and stronger. She'd already spent two years as third officer on a cruise liner.

Kaitlyn had been studying psychology at university and working on her uncle's fairground diner at Canvey Island.

"I'd like to imagine a world where sometimes you're wrong," she sighed.

"Like you've got some sort of feeling for this hood?"

"Some sort of feeling that sometimes you meet someone and there's something special that's not just a load of shit."

"Must have happened somewhere sometime I guess," said Camille.

"But not to me. Not to people like us, women like us."

"I'm a detective. I work on the evidence," said Camille with a laugh. "But, I'd rather work on a cocktail right now."

Kaitlyn took her arm. Tomorrow was a rest day and she could sleep it off.

"Mine's a Mojito,"

"Mine's a Porn Star Martini. These days I've got the glasses to wear with it," said Camille.

They settled with their drinks into a corner of Southsider's Cocktail Club. It was still early evening and the trade was office staff and a few braver tourists taking in South London before dark.

"So, show me what you've done now, my impetuous Kaitlyn."

"It's just a small tattoo. Everyone's got ink."

"Not everyone. Not me. Not the posh lady commissioner of the Metropolitan Police. All those spokesman cops on the TV; they're not inked up."

"I'm a traffic cop grinding it out in the engine room," said Kaitlyn.

"So now you'll have to wear long sleeves. You've fucked your chances for top cop one day."

Of course Camille was right as always. Met Police rules forbade display of tattoos.

"Top cop. I'm a nobody, but I've got some ink that expresses me."

"Bloody show me then."

Kaitlyn slipped off her Nike hoodie top and held out her arm. Camille put on her porn star glasses.

"It's, it's fantastic. Sexy, like too sexy. Makes me think of woman power somehow. Like it's huge. I do love it, but what the fuck is it?"

"It's from a photo I took years ago. It's the Assyrian goddess Ishtar, grand momma of love, fertility, and war."

"That seems to cover most of the angles," commented Camille.

"She also covers desire, political power, and beauty."

"So the tattoo kind of gives you that power?"

"No, women hold that power if they realize it. The picture reminds me, the spirit of the goddess walks with me."

"I'm going to get to the bar and walk some more beautiful spirits back for us," said Camille.

"See? It works," said Kaitlyn leaving her arm bare with a secret pride. She'd been nervous about showing it off. It had changed her, taken her away from being a cop. One day, maybe, the right man would see it, ask her about it and then she'd explain. Explain how she'd gone to the British Museum as part of her psychology course and seen the image, taken a photo. How the idea of such a goddess had spoken to her, seduced her to some extent. And then, maybe the right guy would talk back and ask more, more than just to use her, like she represented that goddess for only him and that her true power was to love in return. Maybe.

"I got doubles. I sense this is going to be a deep exploration," said Camille.

"Explore yourself for once Camille. What's next for you?"

"More of the same. I still see whatshisname on and off."

"You mean like your husband."

"Meaning Captain Fantastic, cruiser of the seven seas, every showgirl dancer, and port of the world."

"Why don't you divorce?"

"What's the point? He needs a lodging between cruises and I need a lodger to help pay the rent. Biologists call it symbiosis."

"You don't care about his private life?"

"I've told him he's a health risk and not to use any of my towels. If he drowns at sea, I get his pension. I keep a close eye on the hurricane forecast and wait for that sad voiced official call, but so far I've not gotten lucky."

"You still love him."

"Not like I'd love a simple gin and tonic."

Kaitlyn got the drinks. Doubles of course. Her mind turned over the wisdom of discussing a certain Randolph Quinn. Her brain said NO. Three double Mojitos slurred YES.

"That guy I put in the cells. I've not met someone like that before," she said, watching Camille's face for her reaction.

"Everyone's a unique individual, just like everyone else."

"No. Listen, he had something special."

"Like a criminal record."

"Could be, but I guess he's a proper banker type."

"And he came on to you?"

"Why wouldn't he?"

"For sure you're gorgeous, hun. The cropped bleached hair, the karate club T-shirt and the tatts. A lot of guys go for that. Your last amour stamped out all the Barbie in you."

"I was never a Barbie. Glen wanted a frilly girl. I tried to please."

"What pleased him was putting you down so you wagged your tail like a whipped pup. He was a mummy's boy monster. So, you've transformed into Miss Ironfist. You know it's not real, not deep down."

"I learned a lot Camille. Is it a weakness to be lonely and just to want someone?"

"For a woman, yes. Love's like a barbecue for a woman. Starts slow, but burns hot. And the end is ashes, just bloody ashes."

"And for the man?"

"He's cooking the meat, hun. Sometimes it burns him, sometimes he gets sick and sometimes it's tough. But a man just keeps on cooking and chewing."

"You're a poet, Camille."

"So you're falling for your cellblock Romeo."

"No, of course not. He got through to me that's all."

Camille called a cab.

"Keep me posted. Don't elope before I've checked him over," she said as she drove away.

Chapter 4

Her cellphone was ringing or maybe it was in her tangled dream. There was light pushing in at the window; she must be awake.

"Kaitlyn Thorn?" asked a female voice.

"Yeah, yeah. Who is this?"

"My name's Shannon Knightsmith. I'm a cop but you don't know me."

"Right now I don't know who I know. What time is it?"

"Just gone eleven o'clock."

Kaitlyn stumbled from her bed. She just about remembered walking the short distance home from the cocktail club.

"Yeah, sorry. I had a late night. It's my day off."

"I know. I wouldn't have called if it wasn't important. I'm chief inspector on the serious and organized crime group; they keep changing our name but it'll always be SO7, Scotland Yard to me."

Kaitlyn fought to clear her head. The woman on the phone had a London accent mixed with something else.

"Well, hi. What?"

"I need to have a chat and it needs to be very soon. What are your plans today and tomorrow?"

"Might check out my stocks and shares and then finish off reading my complete works of Shakespeare. That's after I recover my car from the Battersea Leisure Centre and see if my mum wants me to drive her to the Gala Bingo at Mitcham. I'm not being cheeky but are you on the level or what?"

The woman replied with a laugh in her voice.

"OK. I think you've met a character called Randolph Quinn."

Kaitlyn's heart began to thump in her chest.

"Yeah. Look I locked him up because I didn't really have a choice. I guess he's a big shot banker and he's put in a complaint."

"He's a very big shot banker and he's sure complaining. But, not about you. I'm working from home today and I don't want you to come to Scotland Yard in any case. I'll explain

14

why when I see you. Can you get down the A23 to Fleetworth Green?"

"I know it. It's right on the edge of the Met Police area on Z-district. It's all posh with a stately home, trees and stuff."

"Should take you about an hour. Don't mention this to anyone. Get your car and drive down to the shop in the middle of the village. I'm calling on my own cellphone so you've got my number. I'll meet you there. What's your car?"

"Nissan 350Z."

"I'll spot you. You'll be in time for lunch."

"Is this important?"

"Do you think I'd be calling you to swap pizza recipes?"

Kaitlyn paused for a moment to think. She guessed she could just refuse but on the other hand she was a professional. And somehow a certain Randolph Quinn was in the mix.

"I'll need to get myself together. I'll be there as soon as I can," she said.

"You're a star. Big hug and see you soon."

Kaitlyn took a quick shower. What kind of chief inspector on a flashy Scotland Yard crime squad called you at home and went in for big hugs? This Randolph Quinn must be some kind of big fish in a pretty big pond. For sure he had deep warm eyes and smiling lips that made you just want … and want.

An old Landrover was parked in front of the village shop. Kaitlyn could see a female at the wheel watching her pull up. The driver got out and came back to her window. She was a gorgeous woman, exotic looking, mixed race, with flawless café latte skin. She wore tight riding jodhpurs, Wellington boots and a tweed jacket. At a guess she was about thirty-five.

"I'm Shannon. Follow me."

"You're really a cop right?" asked Kaitlyn, studying her unlikely appearance.

The other woman chuckled, glancing back at Kaitlyn's tattoo, bleached spiky hair and T-shirt design of a painter smashing his easel and canvas with karate blows. The slogan read "Beware. Martial Artist."

"Try me. Ask me a cop question."

"Where's your warrant card?"

She reached into her pocket and pulled out a Met Police ID badge. Kaitlyn flicked her eyes between the photo and the woman's face.

"Do I pass?"

"Let's go then," said Kaitlyn.

The Landrover turned off the road through massive iron gates. A long gravel drive went through woodland until the view opened out into a mowed parkland with a lake. On the other side was a Georgian-style stone mansion which could easily be a royal palace. They stopped in the rear courtyard which housed stables with the heads of tall thoroughbred horses peering out. There was a smell of cooking. Kaitlyn's stomach rumbled as she followed Shannon through a large oak door into a stone-floored kitchen hung with copper pots and strings of onions.

"Is this a police place?" asked Kaitlyn.

"Nah, it's what I call home."

Kaitlyn looked around, bemused by her surroundings. This was nothing like the damp rented house in Battersea she shared with her friend Lucy who worked shifts as a nurse. Even if she were a chief inspector she could never afford this place. She could see that Shannon was following her thoughts.

"I'll explain and then we'll forget this forever. I used to be PC Shannon Aguerri, born in North Peckham. I used to be the village cop here. I married the earl who owns this place. You call me Shannon."

Kaitlyn smiled. She'd heard of this woman.

"You were on the TV. Countess of Crime and all that."

"Yeah, it was a slow news day. No pop stars had died and no cute pandas had been born. They needed a feel-good story."

"I was at Hendon police school then. You did a big crime bust. There was a dead foreign girl…."

Shannon waved her hand.

"That's all old stuff. You're only as good as your last job in this game and your job yesterday was pretty special."

"I did what I had to do and saw it through without exemption," said Kaitlyn.

"And not in a shy way," added Shannon.

"It's my favorite karaoke song, but you've got to be there to catch the full impact."

16

"Next gig I'll be there, Kaitlyn, and that's a promise. There's fresh cooked bread and our own smoked ham."

Kaitlyn stood up while Shannon fixed some lunch. The view from the window was of open fields and miles away in the distance the outline of the heaving urban mass of London.

"So, what do you want? I might not want to do it." She was a very junior rank but she'd deal with this on the front foot.

Shannon looked up from carving generous slices of ham.

"I want you to be a guardian angel to our dear Mr Quinn. I say angel, because angels generally don't end up in bed with their clients. He could charm the apple of temptation from the tree and peel it one handed. You may have noticed that. I can tell you that he sure noticed you."

Kaitlyn's heart pumped air for a second.

"He'd notice any girl."

"Dunno about that. Girls would notice him but from what we can see of him, he's alone."

"Why does it matter?"

"That, my dear Watson, is the question indeed. Listen while you eat."

Shannon sat down. "Randolph Quinn is not a false name. He changed it legally a few years ago. He was a streetwise very sharp guy who tried any way to make money. He even took out a patent on some laser radio system he invented. He had enough cheek to get a job with Sackman-Platinum Bank and has worked his way up to international vice president. That would pay him about one hundred and fifty thousand US dollars a year. There's a big wedge of bonus but there's no figure for that."

"That wouldn't buy his Maserati."

"You're detective material, Kaitlyn. The day job has given him something much more important than a bit of pocket change. It's given him contacts and, believe me, I know just how that feels."

Shannon swept her arm around all of her surroundings.

"It's not what you know but who you know."

"Yeah, and what you know about who you know and who knows what you know," Shannon continued. "Randolph Quinn has the instincts of a stray street dog. He sniffs out dirt even when everything looks clean. He can offer to take care of it, maybe seal it up so the smell doesn't get out. He's a multibillionaire with offshore accounts all round the world. Then one day, someone starts to fret that Randolph might be taking slightly too much commission. Randolph explains that his client is in no position to go to the police or to access accounts when only he knows where they are, the numbers, and the codes. Randolph Quinn is the devil's banker with the key to gangster heaven."

"And that one day was yesterday."

"That was the day they sent him an opening message. No one wants to kill him while he's the only one with the golden key."

"Has he told you all this?"

Shannon laughed.

"If only he would. I can't tell you how we know."

Kaitlyn nodded, looking hard into Shannon's face.

"So you've got an informant or a guy undercover or both, inside the bad guys."

Shannon raised an eyebrow.

"And a humble traffic cop from the trenches is going to put her head in some kind of homicidal lion's mouth?"

"That's my plan, hope, request."

"Why me?"

"Number one, he wants you. Number two you're not a detective with possible links to who knows what…."

"Hey, hold it there," said Kaitlyn. "You're saying you don't trust some of your own team and I'm an innocent clean skin. If you just want a bullet stopper I know some real fat cops who'd soak up a whole magazine."

"When it comes to these guys you can't trust anyone. The fact is we've got nothing on him. We've offered him the full witness protection deal if he comes across. It's just a matter of time before we get enough to lock him up, or the boys get to grab his golden key. We all know that means torture followed by termination."

"Why the hell does he want me? What do you or anyone expect me to do?"

"He wants you, he's a man. You've got the stuff he likes. He thinks you're courageous, daring, and kind."

"Kind?"

"You got him a cup of tea. You didn't have to."

"I liked him, I've got to say that."

18

"He's been on our radar for a couple of years and I talked to him half the night. I like him too but that won't stop me locking him up for twenty years."

Kaitlyn rested her chin in her hands and stared into space. She liked being a traffic cop, the blue lights and sirens drama, the motorcycle outrider duties when they came along. Did she want to help get Randolph Quinn twenty years in jail?

"You can't make me do this, can you?"

"Nope. And I can't overlook that I've already told you too much," said Shannon with a colder tone.

"Fuckin' hell. Fuck, fuck, fuck. OK, tell me what you want me to do."

Shannon reached out and squeezed her hand. I'll be out of sight, but with you all the way. He's still locked up but we've moved him to Paddington Green in a catering van. We can't charge him but we're dragging our feet checking out all his cards. He knows it's a bluff. He hasn't given any statement against the hoods on the bike."

"What's happened to them?"

"One of them had some cocaine the other one was wanted for some petty stuff. We just don't know what happened to the gun. At a guess there was a backup team who mopped up the mess. They're contract boys and in a few days they'll be back on the street. I'm hoping we'll have the resources to keep on top of them."

"When will Quinn get out?"

"When you can get there. We're letting him go on bail on condition he accepts police supervision. The law doesn't give us that power but he knows we'll find some way to bust him if he doesn't play ball. Your job will be to keep close to him. There'll be a team around the periphery and you'll be tooled up. Your firearms scores are top ten percent. The rest—"

Shannon stopped and sighed, giving Kaitlyn's hand another squeeze. "The rest is freestyle for you. We want this guy to come over to the good side, make a deal, and live happily ever after. He doesn't trust cops but he does trust a sparky London girl fallen from the same tree on the same hard ground. If he'll talk to anyone ever, he'll talk to you."

Kaitlyn returned Shannon's squeeze.

"Am I allowed to feel afraid?"

"Who wouldn't? You'll need clothes and your passport just in case. If you can't find it we'll fix it."

"Are we going abroad?"

"He's a top international banker."

"Bloody hell! And who's the enemy Shannon? You owe me an answer to that."

Shannon took a deep breath.

"You're at the point of no return anyway. Yesterday's little crash was organized by a clan of the Albanian Mafia led by a moron called Valmir Rudovic. We're working with the Italian Caribinieri di Milano, the French Gendarmerie in Paris and the FBI Washington DC bureau. This is big. Our estimate is that Randolph Quinn has control of wealth to the value of one hundred and sixty billion US dollars. That's without the legit profits from the investments he makes using his clients' deposits but doesn't want to share."

Kaitlyn sat back in her chair. She was a South London girl; she'd boarded an express train going somewhere so she might as well enjoy it.

"He's a bloody sexy guy," she said with a broad smile.

"Nothing in the police instruction book says you can't enjoy your work," said Shannon.

Chapter 5

Kaitlyn filled her hand luggage suitcase, grabbed her passport, left a quick note about her mother's health for her housemate and called an Uber cab. She had an address in Kensington and a door key. She'd heard of safe houses but never dreamed she'd need one. Everything about this job was bizarre within her own small experience. She'd done two years plodding the beat and then applied to be a traffic cop because she liked fast cars, motorbikes, trucks, trailers and the smell of oil. Her work and life had been on the level. Now she was avoiding police networks and systems, using her own cellphone, anonymous taxis, and telling stories about her mother. It was late September so she wore her hoodie, sweatshirt, jeans, and trainers. As the Uber driver followed his GPS into Courtfield Gardens, London SW5, a choking swirl of smoke made the driver slow. Perhaps some idiot was burning autumn leaves in the park opposite the curve of beautiful Regency-style houses. She smiled to herself. Normally this would be a job for a traffic cop.

The rear passenger door of the car opened just as a tongue of flame flashed across the street in front of them. The cab stopped.

"Just drive mate. Put your foot down and there's fifty quid in your pocket."

Kaitlyn was looking at the breathless form of Randolph Quinn at her side.

"What—?" she began.

"Money solves everything," he said to her with a smile. "Driver, get out onto the Cromwell Road and head back into town."

The guy did as he was told. They sped through the smoke, as flames roared from the basement of a house. Randolph glanced back as he pulled a fifty-pound note from his wallet and pushed it into the driver's shirt pocket.

"I'm as good as my word, mate. Stay calm, keep your mouth shut and you'll get another one."

The balding dark-skinned guy looked back in his mirror, something like terror in his eyes.

"OK, not want problem," he said.

"Me neither. Never play with matches—that's what my mum always told me. Should've listened."

Kaitlyn kept her eyes and ears open as she scrambled to make sense of what had happened. Randolph Quinn was at her side, seemingly untroubled. He turned his warm eyes to her and without any sort of preamble took her hand. His grip was steady, his hand big, strong, but gentle.

"It's cool, we're on top of things again," he said in his deep steady voice.

His touch calmed her, yet sent a jolt into her belly. She was the cop and he was the robber. She had to take command, but the feel of his hand and the control in his manner weakened her will. The back of this taxi was no place to talk. She had to analyze her situation. She'd arrived at a safe house organized by the police. She guessed that Randolph was already there and that something had happened. For sure he would know the story. Now she was in free fall, alone with a guy who was being hunted by the Albanian Mafia. Chief Inspector Shannon Knightsmith had hinted at a problem with police security. Maybe someone on the inside had betrayed the address? God, she was out of her depth. And what the hell should be her next move?

"Get to Harrods Knightsbridge. Go round the back into Basil Street and stop at door 2A," said Randolph.

The driver nodded.

"Harrods?"

"Yeah, I know it's not the sort of place for a girl with your class but it's convenient in the circumstances," he replied.

"Shopping?"

"Why not? Don't you want to look nice tonight?"

"What's happening tonight?"

"Something wonderful. You're going out with me."

He needed a slap. He really deserved a sharp pin in his grinning balloon.

"And if I said no?"

"Then Miss 838 you'd be deserting your official duty and I'd have to speak with your superiors. Don't forget I'm a taxpayer," he said, tracing his hand up her forearm.

The cab stopped. For a moment Randolph stayed seated, checking for trouble in all directions. He handed the driver two fifty-pound notes, stepped out and collected Kaitlyn's suitcase from the trunk.

"What's your name, mate?"

"Tommy, they call me Tommy."

"OK, you're not available for the next hour OK. I'll know if you take a job so don't let me down, Tommy. I don't want you meeting the wrong kind of person. Switch your phone off and get well south of the river before you check in. Do as I say and you're safe, geddit?"

Kaitlyn let him take her hand as the car pulled away.

"This is the left-luggage entrance. Then we can shop," he said.

She didn't answer, but withdrew her hand and took out her cellphone.

"Who you calling?"

"I'm asking the questions, not you," she said.

"Ask yourself this question then. Who can you trust? Your police mates let me out and I agreed to go to a safe house like a good boy. I get inside the door and the neighborhood welcoming committee throw a petrol bomb into the basement. Someone knew where I was going. So who can you trust, my sweet constable Kaitlyn?"

"Lucky I showed up," she said, realizing he was right. With a bit of luck no one knew where they were. All the same she needed to speak with DCI Shannon Knightsmith.

"Just trust me, Randolph."

He turned and stood in front of her, setting down the suitcase. He reached out and held her by the shoulders. His look was calm and strong, holding her eyes in his. *She* was the cop. *He* was the robber. His lips gently kissed her forehead, brushing the bridge of her nose.

"I'll give you back all the trust you put in me. And thanks for calling me by my name."

Oh no. She had closed her eyes and felt his lips, had longed to raise hers to meet with his, longed to respond to him as a woman. Get a grip, Kaitlyn. Get a grip NOW or give up.

"I'm calling my DCI. I trust her."

"That'll be Shannon. I'd have said she was quite a looker if I hadn't already met you."

"What's wrong with you? Can't you see the danger we're in?"

Randolph shielded his eyes like a lookout sailor and made a dumb show of looking up and down the road.

"Damned if I can see any."

She shook her head and pushed the call button.

"Kaitlyn, we were just going to call you."

The voice was Shannon's.

"What's going on? What do I do now?"

"Things are cool. Something went wrong at the house. I know this sounds crazy but don't tell me your location. Are you OK? Are you still with target?"

"Close as a decent girl can get."

"Stick with him and wait for me to call you. You know what I'm saying. I'll call you. Do you understand what I'm saying to you?"

Kaitlyn knew exactly. Someone inside the police had tipped off the bad guys. Shannon knew. Randolph Quinn knew. But no one except the bad guys knew who. Until the good guys did know, she was alone with a dangerous man. And he was a dish to savor.

"For now I'm all you've got, Randolph," she said clicking off her phone.

"You're all I want, Kaitlyn."

"You're some kind of fucking lounge-lizard gangster. I should have just left you for road kill when I had the chance."

"Oooh you're a charmer when you turn it on. Let's stash the case, get you dressed up like a billionaire banker's lady and share the memories of where we're both from with a bottle of champagne. Then we'll dine, then we'll dance, and then you can be my good night cop, watching the baddie sleep while you play up and down with the barrel of your gun."

"What gun? I was supposed to get tooled up at that house."

"No worries," he said sweeping his arms around her waist. "There'll be toothbrushes, pyjamas, and a police issue Glock 26."

"What the fuck?"

"My lovely Kaitlyn, welcome to the world of the infinitely possible. I knew you were coming so I baked a cake."

"The world of infinitely possible cake and death."

"All that bodyguard stuff's your job. I told you I trust you."

24

Kaitlyn let out a long sigh. She could block all this trash if he just didn't have those kind brown eyes and his way of pulling her deeper and deeper into him.

"Randolph, I'll square with you. I'm alone and afraid, OK. You're in some different league to me. Just tell me if you're going to open up and share your whole true story. I'm taking the same risks as you but I'm a nobody. I've got no true home of my own. I've got no money, no power, no big shot career. If you still feel that we're from the same place in life you'll give me a straight answer. Show me that respect or you're on your own, boy."

In a London street a man took a woman in his arms and kissed her lips. That is how it would look to a passerby. To her it was the end of gravity, a floating sense of the serene with a nagging pressure of pleasure in her groin.

"You do have my respect," he said as he held her away for a moment. His gaze was unafraid and confident. His arms were muscular, his face strong but kind. "We'll talk and I won't close any doors. Just push a little when you want to come in."

Chapter 6

Once her suitcase was checked in, he led her to the VIP entrance. The doorman nodded in recognition.

"I see you as sparkly, sapphire blue like your eyes," he said.

"I see me as making my own choices and I don't need another dress or you to pay for it."

"I'm just the guy with the card. Sackman Platinum Bank will pay believe me. Relax Kaitlyn and go with the flow. Just for a while we're free. Things may not always be that way."

There was something serious and maybe sad in his voice that she'd not heard before, something that wasn't a smart-ass quip or joke.

"My job is to keep you breathing and hopefully free. If you want to discuss your options, I'm your girl."

"I know that. You're my girl and I see you as sparkly with sapphire blue for your eyes."

She sighed in frustration. For a moment she'd thought he was going to open up. He beamed a warm smile.

"You said you were my girl, not me. But here's a question. Your DCI Shannon explained the deal, the witness protection and all that stuff. I listened and I didn't say no. I could never trust you guys. Someone knew the address of that house. Work it out for yourself. Imagine you could tip off a guy and earn a million. Tell me there's no one on your team now or in the next twenty years who couldn't be tempted or worse."

"Worse?"

"Cops' kids go to school. Cops' mothers cross the street. Cops have daughters they don't want gang raped. Power is just a politically correct term for ruthlessness. There's guys out there who expect to get what they want and they can't handle disappointment."

What could she answer? He was right. He was too right. Every cop knew crooks that cruised by in limos and laughed at the system. Beyond them were the white collar manipulators of wealth outside the reach of simple cops or judges.

"You can trust me Randolph."

"And I do, my little traffic cop. I can see it in your face. Right now you're part of an experiment. You've got a cellphone and I'm guessing several people know your number. Other people with the right kit can detect your number. With just a simple Whitepage App I can track your phone. Let's see how long it is until someone shows up."

"What kind of someone?"

"My guess could be a cop, a good guy wanting to help. It won't be a Mafia gorilla with a machine gun. They want me alive."

"So what'll be wrong with the cop?"

"He won't be on our side, sugar. He'll be looking to get a better house, stop his wife finding out about his girlfriend or a boyfriend he tried once at school, cover some gambling debts. Everyone's got a list and a history. These days privacy is the one luxury almost no one can buy."

"So I'm adrift with a crook in a sea of crooks."

"When there's sharks in the water it's best to make friends with a killer whale like me and I bet you didn't have a better offer for tonight anyway," he said with a laugh.

She gave a nervous smile in return. She could see what he was doing. He was manipulating her for sure but everything he said seemed plausible. He'd used the term "our side" to mean the two of them. He was blurring the lines gently but steadily. At last her psychology degree was helping out her life. But Oh My God, he'd kissed her. And that kiss had sunken in to her core. *Just play along, Kaitlyn. That's your job.*

"Maybe a bit sparkly," she said.

He threw an arm around her and kissed her cheek.

"Let's play two young shoppers in love. Who's going to interfere with that?" he said.

"Let's play one cop, one crook. If it'll keep me alive I can fake the love."

"I always know if a girl is faking it."

"You're just completely impossible. You think you know about everything, including women."

"Ah, women might be a weak spot. You could help me with that, when you're off duty."

So, when he held out his elbow she took his arm, like a bloody stupid goldfish reacting to food on the surface. She

27

knew it as she watched his eyes go to her hand and then sweep on to her own eyes with a sense of complicity; and triumph. Just his smile sent a teasy ping to her hot spot. She hated her body because it wasn't hers. She could feel she was aroused and loving that warmth. His eyes went to her mouth, his hand came to her cheek, brushed to her chin as she leaned in to him and kissed the soft flesh of his lips. Oh God, she wanted his touch to pluck the ripe fruit of her. She let her breasts press against him, savoring the pleasure. *Oh God, Kaitlyn, what the fuck are you doing?* Once a box of chocolates was open she could never eat just one.

"Now that's what they call method acting."

She stood back and took a deep breath.

"A girl has to rehearse."

He kissed her hairline which was the natural height of his lips.

"This theater never closes," he said.

The escalator took them to the first floor. An immaculately dressed woman of about forty-five smiled with professional assurance and offered her hand to Randolph.

"Mr Quinn, such a pleasure to see you again."

"I'm sorry. I know you guys only do appointments, but my life is very busy."

"We understand your needs, Mr Quinn. We'd always have a personal shopper for you."

"I'd like you to meet my partner, Kaitlyn. She needs…."

"She needs to speak for herself," she interrupted. "I need some clothes because Mr Quinn has taken all of mine away."

The lady raised a questioning eyebrow at Randolph. He laughed.

"I gave them to charity. Kaitlyn has renounced possessions and is entering a convent you see. Tonight is her farewell party."

The woman searched back to Kaitlyn's face and then joined in the laughter.

"Versace. I see you with Italian flair and I believe Mr Quinn is very much associated with Milano."

Kaitlyn nodded. This dame had done her homework, and fast. So this was like being rich.

"Chrissy, I didn't pick up my cell. Could I use your office phone?"

The woman waved and a young male assistant came to escort Randolph. He smiled and walked calmly away. Just what was he on?

"Versace. Shall we take a look?"

"Sure. I guess you know Randolph. He must bring a lot of girls here."

The woman paused as she appraised Kaitlyn from top to toe.

"Never seen him with a girl. You'd never think he was one of the richest men in the world. He likes to buy gifts for clients but I think this is something new and very very exciting. You've got a real look about you—slightly gamin face, full figure but a wiry aura of strength."

"That'll be all those burgers from my uncle's diner on Canvey and my karate," said Kaitlyn.

The lady gave a weak smile and ushered her to a display of fabulous dresses.

"Vair-Sah-Chay, Chianti, spaghetti, Cornetto," said Kaitlyn, almost gasping at the beautiful dresses.

"You have a beautiful Italian accent, madam."

Her eyes fell upon a baroque sleeveless midi dress and widened at the price tag, a mere 2,883 USD. All the same she took it from the rail and gazed at it. It was branded as Wild Side with a slit thigh and gorgeous embroidery. She wanted it. She wanted it. More than that it was sleeveless and would show her tattoo. Then she would know about this guy, then she would be shouting the essence of herself.

"I was just so hoping that would be your choice. May I call you Kaitlyn?"

"Sure, may I try it on?"

She liked what she saw, but her hair was a mess, she'd need shoes and where the hell were they going anyway?

She heard Randolph's voice outside the changing room. This was it.

He stopped talking as he saw her. She did a nervous spin and ended up staring back at him unsteadily. His eyes had fixed on her tattoo as he nodded slowly. Then he opened his arms to her and she ran shoeless the few steps to him.

"You're wild," he said as he held her. "What's the tatt? I love it."

29

"She's Ishtar, Assyrian goddess of love, sex, power, and a bag of stuff."

"Chrissy, we'll need shoes and underwear. Can you do a quick hair fix, makeup and some sparkly sapphire earrings worthy of a goddess?"

"Mr Quinn, this is so strange, maybe fate. We have a beautiful set of Ishtar jewellery by Bee Goddess."

"Sold," replied Randolph.

She'd lost the plot but without orders from above she was just going with the flow. Why fight it? All of this could end in a few blood-soaked seconds. The thought snapped her back to her situation. For a moment they were alone.

"Why did you need to use the phone in their office? You had a cell."

"So I did. I must have left it in that cab with a wiped SIM, just in case someone might be tracking me. Keep your phone on for now. Maybe about now they'll be talking to Tommy. Won't be long until they try a new angle."

"Would they hurt him?"

"Nah. He's no threat to them. Won't hurt to keep alert."

"You cannot live like this forever and for sure I can't."

"Neither of us will have to, believe me."

Apparently this guy had no criminal record. He was a banker not a bank robber. She'd watched him checking out the in-store CCTV. He was ultra aware of surveillance almost like a trained operator. There were big questions about Randolph Quinn and she had no one to ask except him.

It was nearly closing time as they prepared to leave the store with Manolo shoes, Rigby and Peller underwear, the Ishtar earrings, Stella McCartney clutch bag, and immaculate hair and makeup.

"One last thing. Write down all the important numbers from your cell and then wipe the SIM. Here's a Nokia 1100 basic handset. Sackman-Platinum will get you another android."

She thought quickly. She was letting him take charge and she was the cop.

"My DCI has this number. She's going to call me."

As she looked at him a middle-aged suited man approached showing half a smile. She noted his pale blue socks and slip on shoes.

"WPC Thorn, Mr Quinn, thank God you're OK. I'm Detective Sergeant Grant of Special Branch. We've got a police car outside. Please follow me."

Kaitlyn shot a quick glance at Randolph as her karate blow crashed into the man's throat. She followed him to ground and pulled out a vicious looking flick knife from his jacket pocket. Randolph pulled a slick automatic pistol from a shoulder holster and held it firmly aimed at the guy's head.

"What the fuck, Randolph?"

"What the fuck, Kaitlyn?"

She ignored him and spoke to the figure on the floor.

"If you're a cop, I'm a fucking banana. Where's your ID?"

He made no response beyond a few groans. A uniformed concierge had arrived at the scene.

"We'll leave by the VIP exit," instructed Randolph, his gun no longer in sight. This gentleman may need an ambulance, I fear."

Chapter 7

Randolph stepped out and signaled toward a black Chrysler 300 parked up the street. At once the vehicle pulled up alongside them. They slid into the luxurious cushioned leather of the back seat. Randolph took her hand and spoke to the driver.

"You know where to go, André."

"Can we talk?" she asked.

"Sure, you're safe with my team now on a different level. Forget all your worries."

"Forget you've got what looks like a Walther PPK gun in a shoulder holster?"

"Some guys have a man bag. Some guys have a purse for small change. I'm tidy, can't bear a loose gun in my pocket."

"I can't bear some crook with an illegal firearm holding my hand."

"Normally I wouldn't date a girl who'd half killed a cop with a karate chop but hey, we are where we are."

He turned to look at her. His gaze didn't waver. Nothing that had happened troubled him. She was fighting against him. And he was winning. She decided to attack at a tangent.

"That guy wasn't a cop."

"I heard him say he was a sergeant with Special Branch."

"He called me WPC, that's old style stuff off the TV. No Special Branch cop tells you where he's from. And no fucking cop wears slip on shoes just in case they have to put the boot into some villain like you."

"Ouch! That hurt. Maybe the jury will believe no cop carries a flick knife and has a gang name of Cadillaco. If you need a witness call me. If I still love you I'll take the stand."

"You knew him?"

"I'm alive. I know who I need to know."

She sighed and searched for his eyes, all the time squeezing his hand.

"Randolph, just what am I into here?"

"You're in my limo. And we're going to be together for a wonderful evening. You're safe now, my lovely. In this dangerous world you're safe and that's my promise. We've faced dangers together and a force of fate has control of us. Look, you have brought to me a goddess on your arm. We go to a store and they have the jewels made in her name. Sometimes destiny just picks you up. It is bad manners to fight the universe of a man, a woman, and love."

She was fighting. She was fighting. In the leather seats of the limo with this hunk of a beautiful fearless unattached powerful guy she was fighting. Suddenly she felt tearful.

"You bastard. You absolute smooth asshole fucking bastard. Don't let me down that's all."

He reached out and turned her face to look at him. He brushed a tear from her cheek with gentle fingers and brought it to his lips.

"How often does a man meet a truly beautiful woman? How often does he meet a truly beautiful woman he can trust? I take this tear and you have let me take it. I want this taste of you but I'll take nothing you don't give."

"One minute you're barrow boy, next minute you're lounge lizard. What are you?"

"I'm from the same place as you, but wealth and power is a school in itself. Follow your heart and I'll do my best to keep it beating. You've already shown me you'd do the same for me."

She stared ahead as the limo rolled past Buckingham Palace and headed down the Mall towards Whitehall, Trafalgar Square, or the City, and beyond. The streetlights were on but the autumn night was still warm. Did she even want to know where they were going? She had her cellphone but it had been stubbornly silent. He wanted her to wipe the SIM and trash it. It was her last connection to the only world she knew. And yet she knew that somehow it had attracted the last attempted attack. She handed it to him.

"I just need the number for my mum, my friend Camille, and Shannon Knightsmith."

He clicked through her contacts and called out the numbers. She stored them on her new basic phone.

"I'm setting you free, baby. Soon we're going to be so light and free we'll be able to just fly away."

Now the lights were bright against the dusk. They were heading east following the Thames towards the great financial

33

powerhouses of the City and Canary Wharf. Ahead of them was the structure of the iconic and world famous Tower Bridge. André drove smoothly with the defensive style of a professional chauffeur.

"You're a really cool driver. I could learn from you," she said, somehow wanting to bring the game down to a playable level.

"Thank you, madame. I believe you have your own skills. I was trained by the Presidential Republican Guard unit in Paris," replied the chauffeur.

"You're super smooth. I'd like a lesson when you're free. We pro-drivers should stick together."

She could feel the warmth of Randolph's smile like the sun on her cheek. His hand stroked her fingers one by one. She should pull it away and establish control of law and order as the super smooth limo cruised into the soft violet shapeless seduction of the London night. Randolph was speaking in his deep voice.

"We'll go aboard. Call the office to collect the car. I fancy a bit of open sea."

"Open sea?" she repeated.

"England, it's an island. You're never far from the sea," Randolph replied as if this was a normal day at the office.

"Sea?"

"Yeah. It's the other side of Tower Bridge and the Thames Barrier. Once we're aboard I'll fix us both the drink we deserve and you can do whatever beautiful women do. You know all that stuff, not me. I'm going to be staring at a door waiting to see that dress properly displayed. Then we'll eat, then we'll dance, then we'll see what tomorrow brings."

The car was pulling up on the quay next to HMS Belfast, the famous museum battleship. The driver had sprung out and was opening her door. In the distance she could hear piano music, smoochy jazz that just hooked you and melted into your soul like sucked dark Belgian chocolate. Randolph eased his hand into the small of her back and directed her along the dock. A powerful motor launch with uniformed crew was waiting at the foot of some steps. He steadied her as they boarded. The boat pulled away, passing under the bow of the huge gray warship. Moored alongside was a white vessel, maybe even longer. In the side of it was an illuminated open space, like a garage. The launch slid into the belly of the huge white ship. At once the hull closed and a series of engraved glass doors opened into a fabulous marble-floored atrium with palm trees, paneled wood, and waiters in bow ties.

She hoped her mouth hadn't hung open like some dolt.

"What is this? Where am I?"

Even the questions seemed dumb, but how could such things exist?

"You're on board the Platinum-Demeter, my personal yacht."

"It's a bloody liner."

"Not quite, but she's big enough. I hope you don't mind but we're setting sail at once. London's a bit hot for me at the moment and I prefer the neighbors on the high seas."

"Well, where the fuck are we going?"

"I've got some business in Milan. Venice is a convenient port, and I keep a very special Ferrari there. Just maybe I'll let you drive."

"My passport is at Harrods in my suitcase," she said realizing that that was the least of her worries.

"Your suitcase is in your room. I had it collected while we were shopping."

"You can't just take me over and assume I'm going to play along."

"I'm just cooperating with the authorities, Kaitlyn. Your boss told you to stay close and pump me for information didn't she? You can't deny it. You've not even switched your pump on yet, and bosses always want results. Just do your duty, constable."

"I don't do plumbing."

"Good job I don't leak then," he said taking her by the hand to the elevator. "It'd be such a cliché to kiss a girl in here."

"Then keep your gob to yourself. The next scene in the film is where they lose track of space and time, the doors open, and there's a crowd gawping at the show."

"Not in my personal suite, I hope."

His lips felt for hers, his eyes closed when she peeped. This time his hand touched the side of her breast, the pressure sending that same ping to her groin. She let him draw her tight against him. He had a slight smell of the day, of male. The

35

elevator door opened. She took a breath but kept her eyes on his face.

"Don't tell me there's a crowd and they're about to applaud," she said.

"There would have been but this is a budget movie. I couldn't afford the extras and the champagne."

She turned as he smiled and led her by the hand into the room. A magnum of champagne waited on a beautiful antique table.

"OK, I'm just a regular corny billionaire. I have to watch gangster movies to know how to behave. The guy gets the gorgeous yet unobtainable woman and offers wine. Then she realizes maybe she could want him, it all goes misty and they start singing."

Kaitlyn smiled. She had to. She just had to. She struck a pose.

"Hoo, like a virgin. Touched for the very first time. When your heart beats next to mine," she sang.

"Wow!"

"I'm karaoke cop. You've been warned."

She was pleased to have asserted an ounce of her own style. What a room. Thick pile cream carpet, chandeliers, chocolate brown buttoned leather sofa, paintings she guessed were old master Italian style with cherubs and rich noble types. An intercom was buzzing gently on the wall.

"We'll fill our glasses and go along the corridor for a moment. They're opening Tower Bridge for us. I love it. It reminds me of going through the turnstiles to watch soccer at Selhurst Park when I was a kid."

He popped the cork of the Pol Roger Cuvée Winston Churchill vintage champagne. She took a sip, then a gulp. It was delicious and complex. Almost at once the hit went to her brain and belly. Her last meal had been lunch with DCI Shannon Knightsmith. Another glass of this golden thrill of temptation and she'd be letting go.

They took their drinks through a door to a darkened room with uniformed officers, sweeping radar screens, a ship's wheel held by a sailor. The view ahead was of Tower Bridge, illuminated against the night. Reflections rippled in the dark current-dappled water. Slowly the bridge started to open.

"This is power. Now this is fucking power," she said.

And how she loved it. How it was not to be an ant struggling endlessly against the world. How this power went with the champagne. A waiter was at her side with the bottle.

"May I?" he inquired nodding at her empty glass.

"You bet."

The huge ship eased itself through the bridge. Straight ahead stood the tall quirky-shaped skyscrapers of Canary Wharf with illuminated signs of the world's greatest banks. By far the biggest was Sackman-Platinum.

"Impressed?" he asked.

"Yeah, who wouldn't be?"

"I'll show you your suite. All your clothes are prepared. Then we'll eat."

He opened a wood-paneled door. The smell was of perfume, maybe flowers. Her clothes from Harrods lay neatly on a golden silk-covered king-size bed. He stroked his hand down her cheek.

"I'll leave you now because I can be a very naughty boy sometimes. You must be hungry and you do need to eat. Our bellies are from the same London kitchen. I bet if I like it, you'll like it."

"How do I find you again or am I on CCTV?"

"Go through that door in the corner. Don't forget to give me a twirl as you come in."

Chapter 8

For a moment she sat on the edge of the bed. The perfection of the silk shocked her even through her half-drunk, befuddled senses. There was something she just had to do although she had been ordered not to. She hit the call button on the unfamiliar cellphone.

"Who's this?" said the voice of DCI Shannon Knightsmith.

"It's me, Kaitlyn Thorn. I know you told me not to call, but I haven't got fifty options."

"Look, you've done the right thing. I've been calling you over and over."

"I've had a phone change. Shannon, it looked like the bad guys, whoever they are, were tracking me. I've stuck with Randolph Quinn but I'm clueless now."

"I'm so sorry, Kaitlyn. Someone inside our unit must have tipped them off. Believe me we're turning over every stone but right now we can't trust anyone."

"Cool, I'll just hang in here on his personal yacht. As far as I know we're on our way to Milan via Venice. I guess you're OK with signing off my overtime pay. I haven't got much jurisdiction as a cop once I'm out of UK waters."

"I can live with that. The boat is on satellite surveillance so we won't lose you. Has he opened up at all?"

"Too early to tell. I'll know better after dinner if we pop another bottle of champagne. He's one hell of a generous guy."

Her thoughts focused briefly on the small matter of his illegal possession of a firearm. For now the boss didn't need to know small details.

"I've got your number now. Stay with it, Kaitlyn."

"It's tough, but someone's got to do it. Gotta go, duty calls," she replied.

So, she'd checked in with the boss and she was a working girl pleasing the system. Better get changed and not forget the twirl.

She knew she looked good. The sapphire and diamond earrings sparkled in the light from the chandelier. The ring glinted on her finger. The dress was a perfect fit, the slash running just high enough up her thigh to provide an interested man with a glimpse of her lace trimmed panties. Was she allowing herself to be seduced by wealth, power, and sexual desire? Could her integrity be so easily put at risk? Too damned right it could and she knew it. She looked good, the champagne was a dream and Randolph Quinn was gorgeous. It was time to go through that door.

For a moment he didn't speak. His hair was still wet and even darker, swept back with an aristocratic insouciance. He had changed into a white shirt accentuated by his tan. A Hermes belt held up his black Zanella handmade trousers. She held his eyes before executing her twirl.

"So, so lovely," he said with an astonished simplicity. "I thought you'd scrub up well, but you didn't need much on top of what you've got. But bloody hell, how am I gonna keep hold of a girl like you?"

"First you'll have to get hold of me at all."

He took a couple of strides and pulled her into his arms. His kiss was as if their lips had once before been molded in the history of a man and a woman. It was a finding of place, some place that you would always crave once you knew it existed. A helpless pulse buzzed in her groin. She let him hold her thrilling spot to the hard muscle of his thigh. She was hot and wet, feeling almost too close, far too close. He groaned a little as her belly pressed into his powerful erection. If he ran his hand now up her bare thigh she would come as they kissed with wet searching tongues. She was holding herself tight, feeling his hard cock pushing against her. She was just holding that pleasure, just too long, couldn't hold back thinking of his cock jetting his juice into her as she came. She played a hard-core fantasy of him jerking off, helplessly pulsing out his sperm. He held her tight in support as she convulsed against him. My God, she'd just let go. She must be gushing as she growled out the last spasm of her ecstasy into his mouth and onto his softly kissing lips.

"That was so beautiful, such a compliment to a man to think someone so lovely would find pleasure in him."

39

"I, I, I sort of wandered off into the long grass," she said.

"I'll have to fix up some sort of safari on a really big savannah," he said with his warm smile. "We need to eat and think about our situation."

She took a deep breath. Bloody hell, she'd just come kissing him. Maybe he hadn't realized. Teasy aftershocks still flickered in her own little shaft. His hand ran down across her breasts to her waist. He led her to the door and out onto a swish dining deck with panoramic views and a glass-domed roof. The lights of the coast were sprinkled along a dark horizon.

"That's Canvey Island and Southend. We're at anchor in the Thames Estuary. Unless the bad guys have got warships or submarines we can relax here."

She took in the view. They were at the top of the enormous ship.

"I used to sell burgers at my uncle's fairground diner on Canvey Island," she said.

He nodded and smiled, pulling her to him.

"We're from the same pod, ain't we? I love the old fairground stuff, the rides, the fried onions, the rifle range sideshows and the cuddly toys. I always dreamed a lovely girl would be on my arm one day and I'd win her the prize teddy. Pity we can't go ashore."

He spoke in his normal cheeky way but with an edge of sadness. She pushed her fingers back through his hair and looked up into his eyes.

"You could take a girl to a fair, surely."

"If I could find the right girl and if my life could ever be normal."

"Like not being a billionaire on the run from the Albanian Mafia. If you want to talk about your options, I'm your girl."

He tweaked his eyebrow, but didn't answer.

"One day we'll have caviar and lobster thermidor, but tonight I've just ordered a couple of big rib eye steaks. Don't tell me you don't like fries."

They took a window table while waiters brought them their meals. The steak was rich and soft. He poured generous glasses of red Chateauneuf du Pape. She took a slug of smooth heaven. Added to the champagne, the wine swept aside her reserve and focus.

"So, Randolph just bloody well tell me why you want me here?"

"I saw you and liked what I saw. I said to myself here's a brave girl who's out on her own in a cop car, turning up at whatever happens next. How many girls do you think are interested in billionaires?"

"Dunno, might be a few old slappers I suppose. Generally a sweet virgin like me wouldn't be interested."

"And that's why I want you. Kaitlyn, you're fucking gorgeous and you know it."

"I want you to know I play Bingo with my mum, I get drunk and sing karaoke, and, and. And I'm starting to really care about you and I'm fucking terrified that you're going to hurt me."

She blew out her cheeks. She was a bit drunk and just saying what she thought. She had never been made to play girl games. He reached out and took both of her hands in his.

"Hurt you? You're afraid of that?"

"Yeah. Simple. I get swept up in you and you soon see the real boring deal. You won't want any commitment like all the bloody rotten bastards and users, and I'm there with my fake smile saying I understand. Look Randolph, it's the wine talking, but shit I don't care. I should never just open up like this, but I'm afraid of my own helplessness if I want a guy. I know it's not hip or feminazi to tell you that but that's how I am. Maybe that's why I shoot guns, do karate, drive fast cars."

His eyes were on her face, their kindness almost a caress.

"And why you have that tattoo of Ishtar on your arm maybe?"

She nodded. Had she ever truly thought about the reason?

"She represents female power, but a lot of that power is in the idea of giving love too. It says I'm someone, not a cop. It says I'm all sorts of stuff."

He turned her arm to see the whole design. He leaned across the table and gently kissed the figure at the groin.

"I can't say I'll *never* hurt you. All I can say is that I won't ever hurt you by turning away from you."

"How the hell can you just say that about the future?"

"Because I'm the kind of guy who knows what he wants. If I hadn't known the future how would I have known you'd want a steak? My powers are supernatural."

41

"Your powers are barrow boy bullshit crook."

"And your powers are burger-flipping karaoke girl."

He shrugged and held her eyes.

"OK, we're just two black and white biographies fallen from Facebook into each other's arms. Face value's the only sensible price if you don't want to spend too much. Doesn't mean we can't dance, I guess."

He made a sign and a guy started to play a piano in the far corner of the room. The tune was silky and familiar. She had to. She bloody well had to sing.

With a song in my heart
I behold your adorable face
Just a song at the start
But it soon is a hymn to your grace....

His eyes softened in a way she'd never seen a man react as she sang the song remembered from her father's vinyl Ella Fitzgerald collection when she'd dreamed of being a real singer, not a girl's night karaoke queen. She hung onto the notes, watching him grip his bottom lip in his teeth, almost as if he was fighting to hold back emotion.

She finished the song as the piano guy stood up to applaud. Randolph was simply laying his eyes on her face and watching her lips.

"So beautiful. You really can do it, can't you? You could steal a heart from a man, roast it, carve it for his dinner, and he'd be begging for more."

"That's one hell of an image."

"Worked as a butcher's boy as a weekend job," he said.

She smiled. She'd caught him by surprise and he'd changed the mood so as not to show his soul. Maybe, just maybe, he'd been hurt too.

The piano re-started. And there on the dark sea with the land of all their dangers held away for this one night they danced, often lips to lips, threatened only by the terror of love.

Chapter 9

It was 2 a.m. Too late to be in his bedroom, watching him undress, the shirt slipping from his broad, muscular shoulders. This guy had the build of a fighter. He hadn't dragged her there, hadn't made her sit on his bed to watch the show. God, he had already made her come in her panties with a kiss. Much more of this and she'd have to deal with her issues herself. He ran his hand over the hard flat muscle of his stomach, letting his fingers stray down under his belt where the first hint of his pubic hair teased up onto his tanned skin. His fingers were at the buckle. *Kaitlyn, it's only sex, it's only pleasure,* she told herself. He was watching her, letting her know that he knew where her eyes were fixed.

"It kind of gets personal in a minute," he said with a slow smile.

She kicked off her shoes and lay back on the bed, propping herself up on the pillows, wantonly showing her panties.

"I did the cabaret, you do the striptease," she answered, feeling the excited pulse of her lust in the depth of her belly.

He smiled back, flicking off the buckle and stepping out of his pants. Now he stood before her, his hard cock bursting from his white briefs. Her eyes shot to the slight darkening of the fabric where his man juice had already started to flow. She felt evil, wicked. She let her hand drift to her pouting hot groove. His eyes widened as his own hand slid to his cock. Her fantasy was of his semen pulsing into her hot tube. She closed her eyes, let the image take her. Oh God, he was pulling away her panties, his tongue was teasing and urging her on. She opened her eyes to see his head buried in her groin as the jolts of orgasm doubled her over onto him. For a second she subsided, allowed the tease to build without holding herself tight to bring it on. She looked down again. He was licking her, conscious of her climb to her summit, and jerking his own massive cock. His fingers eased inside her as his tongue drew her on and on. Her own hands went to her nipples sending the final sparks of release to her clitoris. She was letting go without abandon, animal sounds expressing the jungle of her woman soul and lust. His hot cock filled her as she was coming and then built her again to some higher peak from which she could only crash like a massive wave. She heard his deep voice urging her as his hard cock drove in to the limit of her flesh. Her own hand reached for her clitoris. She had to catch his wave as he groaned out his release into the heat of her flesh. She caught that same wave, calling out into the blur of desire and coming, coming, coming into the shallows of a tender kiss and the opening of eyes to see the gaze of love returned.

He didn't move, didn't turn away but kept his eyes steady on her face. His voice was slow and deep.

"At last I've made love with a woman."

She smiled.

"You've made love to plenty of girls, Mr Quinn."

"I said made love *with*," he replied.

"I guess not too often on the first date. I imagine it's no use saying I'm not that sort of girl if we assess the evidence."

"It's not our first date. You invited me back to your police cell, gave me a cup of tea without even a kiss and left me alone all night and I could have done with your company believe me."

He lay on his back, pulling her to rest her head on his chest, his arm around her. She'd just forgotten everything she knew about men, about being a cop, about every kind of risk. In the warmth and the illusion of safety in his hold she didn't care. She simply didn't care.

"How is it with a man and a woman? Is there someone for you, for me, for all the lonely people? Is it someone special or just someone half decent who's there at the right time?" she said.

She felt the physical vibration of his voice as he answered.

"You're a strange one. Don't girls want to think in terms of love? I'll be honest, Kaitlyn, I'm asking the same question since I met you. I know what I want the answer to be, but right now I've got a bit of business hanging over me. Is it fair of me to ask you to stay with me and trust me?"

"No, it's not fair."

"That's the right answer."

"But life isn't fair, so I guess that if I *did* stay with you and *did* trust you that'd be accepting the way life is—not fair, but life."

He pulled her tighter to his body.

"You seem an educated girl, I'm guessing you studied logic at university."

"Psychology as it happens. I guess you did economics."

"I did car cleaning and got to sell a few. I got a job in a factory making parts for medical lasers. One day I noticed my cellphone changed tone when a laser was being tested. I did some experiments and found I could speed up the phone signal. One day I read about bankers making millions just because they could buy or sell faster. I phoned a bunch of banks and asked to talk to the top man. Every single one told me to fuck off. One day I read about a lady who broke all the rules to be a big Wall Street gambler. She kind of gave me a job.

"A lady?"

"Yeah, the CEO of Sackman-Platinum is a sweet little girlie just like you. She invited me for an interview and we clicked. She's a smart woman."

"Do I want to know about your relationship?"

"Maybe not. She was just a regular millionaire in those days. She even had a mortgage on her castle in France. She's in a different league now."

"And did you, you know, take over the handling of her assets?"

He sighed.

"Stella Boursellino enjoys the company of young people. She quickly saw my financial talents and exploited them."

"She's a super-rich cougar with an itch that needs scratching," said Kaitlyn, imagining this business-suited power bitch.

"She's a woman. She has needs and weaknesses like all the world, like you, like me."

"But you slept with the boss."

"Kaitlyn, this moment here is about you and me now. Let's say I respect and admire her as a person in business and in her life. She's in a relationship with a good guy. I won't ever ask you to list the abandoned lovers and broken hearts that fan out behind you."

"How old is she?"

"Today she is fifty-two."

"You know her birthday don't you. You'll think of her that day, won't you?"

"Kaitlyn, I'm talking about her only because I don't want to be dishonest. You're giving me vibes you're a jealous girl."

"Too right, I am."

He propped himself up on an elbow and looked into her eyes.

"Here with you now I'm as happy as I've ever been. While you're at my side and on my side, the old green-eyed monster can stay in its cave. That's a promise you can bank."

She stroked his hair back and smiled. She knew she had no right to batter him over what may have happened before she'd met him. In her heart she knew that simple fact wouldn't stop her. He hadn't said he'd slept with this sophisticated wealthy woman of the world with at least one castle somewhere. If he denied it she wouldn't believe him anyway. It was just so fucking obvious. He'd walked into her office with that smile, that look, those hands, those shoulders and the cheek of the devil himself. She could see her, perfectly dressed and poised, pushing back her executive chair, slowly crossing her tanned waxed legs. *Kaitlyn, stop this now!* And another thing. This woman was in the same business. Maybe she lit the log fire at her castle with bundles of dirty money.

"I'm trying not to think about you touching someone else like you've just touched me."

"Look, my lovely woman, I've never wanted to touch a woman in the way I've touched you. I want you to stay, to be with me."

She let out a long breath. Her over-intensity was not his problem and it had caused her enough pain already.

"I'm just a cop and I'm on your case, Randolph Quinn."

He took her cheeks in his hands, easing her lips toward his tender searching kiss.

"You've got me locked up, officer. Don't hide the key anywhere sexy. I might find it, and I don't want to escape."

"You're assuming I'll let you look for it."

His hand brushed across her belly. She groaned helplessly. He had her key.

46

Chapter 10

OK, she was waking up in bed with the guy she was supposed to be guarding and interviewing. How many times had he loved her? A mellow marshmallow sense of fulfillment rocked her as this gorgeous loving man spooned into her back, his arm over her and soothing her breast. There was someone else in the room. Fuck! What the fuck was some guy doing?

"Sir, Mr Quinn. A message from London, urgent."

She sat up to see a uniformed steward shaking Randolph by the shoulder.

"Sir, kidnap Signora Boursellino. Captain says, come quick. Need orders, sir."

Randolph jolted into consciousness.

"What's our position?" he snapped out.

"English Channel, sir, near Brighton."

"I'll be there in five. Prepare a fast launch and the chopper. Tell Captain Fuller I'll need a briefing in the conference room."

Kaitlyn watched him leap from the bed, already wide awake. This was a weird guy—part commando, part Casanova, part billionaire. God, he was sexy.

"What's going on? You gonna shower or what? You'll stink of sex," she said.

He smiled as he threw on jeans and a jumper.

"Great, then I'll be reliving what real woman-love can be all day."

Kaitlyn began to compute what was happening. That very same Stella, seemingly Randolph's boss, had been kidnapped. Looked like a job for the cops.

"What are you planning to do? The police won't want you on some sort of vigilante mission," she said.

"I can't imagine the police will be aware of it. Get some clothes on if you want to see some action."

She found her jeans and hoodie top. It didn't seem there was time for showers. She took her place next to him in a long-tabled state room with windows looking out on the sea. She could just see the south coast of England in the far distance. A bearded naval officer with a lot of gold on his epaulets entered with a handful of papers.

"Good morning. I'm Captain Will Fuller," he said, reaching out to shake Kaitlyn's hand. "Sir, Madame Boursellino was seized from her car as she pulled up outside the Ritz Hotel in Paris at about 1:30 this morning. Two men wearing balaclavas and armed with light machine guns held up the chauffeur and the bodyguard. There was an exchange of fire and the guard was killed. They shot out the tires of the car to prevent a pursuit. A demand has been received at the New York HQ of Sackman-Platinum.

"What do they want?" asked Randolph.

"Sir, they want you to surrender to them in exchange for Madame Boursellino. I believe you know these gentleman wish to discuss matters of business with you."

Randolph glanced at the array of wall clocks showing all the time zones of the world. His face was serious and thoughtful.

"OK, I'll agree to that of course. I'll need André and two sets of kit in tourist-style rucksacks."

"Stella, Madame Boursellino, was wearing her GPS tracker watch. It looks as if they haven't spotted it because it's still monitoring her heartbeat. We have an exact fix in a restaurant in La Rue de la Huchette on La Rive Gauche."

"Where do they want me to meet them?"

"We don't know. They've provided a French cellphone number. You call it and you take it from there."

Kaitlyn's heart was thumping. Randolph was about to get mixed up in some sort of drama involving Mafia-style killers with machine guns seemingly on the streets of Paris. She'd never even been to France.

"I can't get involved in this," she said, as his eyes flicked to hers.

"You're involved. I'm not under arrest or under your jurisdiction in any way. Here's the bottom line, Kaitlyn. These bastards will rape and torture Stella before they kill her. If we tell the French police where she is, they would go in with grenades and tanks. If we don't get her out, she doesn't get out."

"I'm not part of this 'we.' I'm a Metropolitan Police London traffic cop. I operate within the law."

"And I'm a banker. You've not broken any laws yet anyway. Just come along as a neutral observer. By the way, you look lovely even first thing in the morning."

She watched his calm handsome face. He had no fear. Just what sort of banker was he? Sure he did business with crooks and killers but she guessed that half the world of finance was a billionaire's laundromat for crime of some sort. Her own world had lost its roots and reality and this man had the courage and daring to confront life and force it to be how he wanted it. All she'd ever done was played to the system, been the good girl, jumped the hoops for fear of being rejected, of disappointing others. That was the girl she was beginning to recognize and dislike when she'd gone for that tattoo. Ishtar, goddess of power, love, and combat. She didn't have to hurt anyone. Life was throwing her a chance, a chance that had teased her since she'd discovered the history of that woman-god and proclaimed her power on her own flesh. She'd meant it as a badge of intent. Now, now, and now *and now,* she'd walked to the edge of the diving board.

She nodded, conscious that she was learning something about the nature of fear. Now she had decided; she was calm. The micro-distance between the hero and the coward is nothing but the infinite void of indecision.

"It's a fucking good job you're so bloody good-looking. Let's go," she said.

He smiled slowly.

"Good girl. Soon as I met you I could see your character. I'd trust you beyond most operators I've known. And of course, there is your troubling beauty, but I can cope with that."

For a second she bridled at the "good girl," but she let it slip. What did he mean by operator? He was speaking to Captain Fuller.

"Full speed for the French coast. Kaitlyn, there'll be time to get a shower so you can get on with that. Trainers, jeans, hoodie, that's the dress of the day."

"Am I dismissed, sir?"

"For now. Stand by for further orders," he replied with a laugh.

This guy was so up himself, so arrogant, so competent and courageous. At least she'd be able to call DCI Shannon Knightsmith.

It felt good to be clean and made up as the number rang.

"We know where you are by your ship's transponder. We've had a report from the Parisian police department of a shooting at the Ritz involving an employee of Sackman-Platinum. Eye witnesses say that a woman, maybe drunk, was literally dragged out of a car but they've had no reports of anyone missing. They're asking us because our interest in Randolph Quinn is flagged up on the Interpol database. I'm just watching your trace now and I can see you've changed course toward the French coast."

"I thought we'd increased speed. Everything seems calm here."

Shit, Kaitlyn—what the fuck are you doing? Some instinct had told her not to give away what they were doing. Some instinct that had made her lie to her boss, a top Scotland Yard detective. She trusted Shannon but someone on the inside had already betrayed the operation. She'd lied and she was stuck with it. "I'm just playing along and keeping my eyes and ears open. He's promised to let me know everything if I just give him a bit of space."

She'd lost it. Now she was in fantasy land with no hope of getting out. *Why are you doing this to yourself, Kaitlyn?*

"He'd promise you the world if it'd make him a dollar, but you're doing a brilliant job. Don't put yourself at unnecessary risk. Stay as close as you can. I've got a suspicion we've got a kidnap-type situation to put some squeeze on Randolph's smooth-talking throat. That's just my cop intuition."

"So what if we end up in France or some other place like Paris?"

"Just don't get involved with gangsters, guns, or the cakes. Definitely avoid the cakes if you want to keep your shape."

Kaitlyn could hear the smile in Shannon's voice. She was a great boss and she didn't deserve to be lied to. Too late, she'd chosen her path, so get on with it.

"OK. No cakes. Shannon, this guy Randolph; is he bad all through?"

"Whoa! We're only after the criminal bits of him. The smile, the looks he'll still have those in jail, my little darling innocent. Yup. He's a bad guy. Geddit? We cop. Him crook. When this is over you're going to be a Scotland Yard detective and you'll never ask that kind of question again, believe me. Just stay close and have a lovely day."

She turned off the phone and looked at herself in the mirror.

"You cop. Him crook. You good. Him bad. Geddit. Geddit."

"Well, what a way to thank a man for offering you a trip to Paris."

Randolph must have come in from his adjoining room as she'd been speaking to Shannon. He took her in his arms. "Thanks for your trust in me. You could have blown the whole deal."

"Then why didn't you tell me not to call her?"

"I knew you would call in. I decided to give you that opportunity and also decided to have the bridge monitor the content. If you'd had an attack of Robocop honesty we'd have cut the satellite link. Now I know your heart. I didn't ask you to lie to your boss but you did it for me."

"I did it because I'm not sure who to trust and that, Mr Quinn, includes you."

"Then I'll have to prove things with actions not words, won't I?"

"You will."

Her answer blurred into his kiss. She'd boarded the fairground ride and she couldn't get off until it stopped. And another thing. If she got involved in some mission to rescue the silken sophisticated Signora Stella Boursellino, the rich seductive cow would forever be in a debt she could never repay. Sometimes Kaitlyn really didn't like herself. How could she loathe some pampered gorgeous bitch she'd never met?

Chapter 11

The chopper lifted off from the deck as the door closed. André, the chauffeur she'd met was already aboard alongside the casually dressed pilot. Randolph handed her a blue Adidas rucksack. She peered inside and took a sharp breath.

"I hope it's the model you like. It's the regular Glock 26 you guys train with."

"I don't want to be carrying any sort of firearm."

"It's loaded so be careful," he replied, ignoring her comment. "Transfer it to your hoodie and get the feel of it. I'm sticking to my Walther PPK. OK, there's a balaclava, leather gloves, and a few useful gadgets like plastic tape, a dagger, and a claw hammer. You've got the Semtex and I'm carrying the cellphone-activated detonator. I'm a strict follower of the Health and Safety rule book."

"This is crazy. Where did you get this stuff?"

"Amazon Prime—it's well worth the fee. They don't just do box set romance you know."

"Fuck off, Randolph. I didn't sign up to this. What the fuck are you?"

"I'm an international vice-president of a major Wall Street bank. We keep the same level of technology as our clients. In business it's never a good move to be behind the curve."

"Gangsters?"

"Wall Street."

"Gangsters."

"City of London."

She wasn't going to win with him. She didn't have to open fire or plant a bomb. She was building a watertight case against him. Yes, for sure, that was what she was doing. *Stay calm, Kaitlyn. You're only doing your duty.*

Within a few minutes they were hovering seven or eight feet above what looked like a car park. André slid back the door and jumped. Randolph nodded for her to go next. She landed and sprang clear. The engine of the chopper roared as the machine swooped away low over the roofs of office buildings and shops. She caught a last sight of Randolph waving from the window.

André was walking away, waving back for her to join him. A few French citizens eyed them curiously.

"Fucking hell. He's just flown off. I'm supposed to be with him," she said.

"He has a meeting. Mr Quinn did not want to risk your life. Anyway we have a maiden to rescue."

"What—you and me? This is crazy. I'm in Paris, I suppose, armed to the teeth with some guy I don't know. Randolph's tricked me and now I'm supposed to be rescuing his ex-mistress, lover, or whatever."

"I told him you wouldn't be pleased," said André with a shrug.

"Well, just like your fucking boss it looks like you're always right. Yes, I'm not in any way one bit fucking pleased."

"I have both the rucksacks. We're heading for the RER rail station and then it's ooh-la-la Pareee."

Ahead of them was the entrance to a kind of subway station. She tried to pronounce the name *Emerainville Pontault-Combault*, merely to distract herself from her terror and, she had to admit, anger. André was laughing.

"Madame has an unusual accent," he said.

"No wonder your bloody language hasn't taken over the world. Look, I'm out of here. I'm not going anywhere with you. My job is with Randolph. I'm going to get to a British Embassy or something like that and you can't stop me."

"I understand. Madame, may I call you Kaitlyn?"

"Just get on with it."

"Randolph himself is going into a dangerous situation. He has to make these guys believe he's surrendering to them. These are very nasty boys, you understand. He has to hang there as visible bait while we get our target out. He will risk his own life one hundred percent to save her, I know this."

"This is ridiculous. Why the fuck should I care if he dies for some old cash bag witch?"

"You would not be saying this if you knew her as I do. She is always a very beautiful woman. If we don't get her out she will die, after the usual gang rape and torture of course. I know that ladies can be very jealous of another woman but as a police officer I know you would be above those ideas. Mr Quinn's relationship with Stella is very complex and not what you think perhaps."

"So let's call the French police, gendarmes, or whatever and let them handle it."

"You are certain that every single officer can be trusted? These bad guys are some of the richest people in the world. When criminals get this power all the regular boundaries are gone. This is Silicon Alley. They know who searches what on the Internet, they know who buys the porn, who's got a disease he doesn't want to mention to his life insurance company. They've even got the DNA sample you sent off to that ancestry website. This is like an octopus with eyes and ears the length of every tentacle."

"And Sackman-Platinum Bank makes them look like yum yum calamari in a regular seafood cocktail."

André nodded.

"This much is true. This part of the world I cannot change. I am thinking of a woman alone and afraid, hoping and hoping someone will help her. That is all."

"Christ, André, where do you guys get all this heartbreak stuff? Don't tell me on Amazon. Just tell me what you want me to do."

He smiled.

"Randolph was right about you."

"I know, and Randolph is always right about everything."

"He is going into a tiger's cage alone. No one can be right all the time."

His tone was grave and considered. This lovely man who had reached into her was going to die, wasn't he? He had trusted her to carry out a mission for which he himself was prepared to give up his life. She felt a surge of emotion.

"André, I don't want him to die. I, I...."

Her tears choked the end of her words.

"Then maybe he has your heart and with two hearts he has twice the chances. His best chance is for us to do a good job and get the timing absolutely right. Once Stella is free he can act as he sees best. We mustn't fool ourselves. Randolph's life will be in our hands. No more tears, no emotion. Timing and hard steel nerves are our only friends for now. We have the high ground. We know where she is and they don't know that we know. That's why we're going in alone. And just maybe the regular cops wouldn't be using plastic explosives."

Her heart thumped. There was something about this guy that she trusted. She'd seen him drive, knew that he'd trained with the French Presidential Guard. He had to be a SEAL or SAS type. He was about forty, compact and stocky. He wore a leather biker-style jacket and no fashion-style loose jeans with turn-ups. His trainers were no regular brand but at a glance had steel toecaps. His hair was cropped, both his brows scarred, his nose off center. His hands were strong looking and his wrists broad. She didn't know where he'd been but at a guess, wherever he had been, he'd made an impression. A few dead leaves chased around her feet in tiny whirlwinds. Autumn was wiping its wet feet on the doormat of winter. Time to go.

The train rattled through the suburbs of Paris. They made a change onto the metro at Gare du Nord and whooshed under the River Seine to Saint Michel Notre Dame. Once out on the street André hailed a Parisian taxi. He handed the driver a Sackman-Platinum credit card, spoke quickly in French and shook the driver's hand. She had no idea what had gone on but it had to be expensive. She tried not to think about what she'd agreed to do. Not that she knew! She saw the street sign Rue de la Huchette. It looked like a whole street of Greek restaurants, bars, pizza joints, and tourists. André was calm, but tight and watchful.

"Take my arm, like you're my beautiful student daughter from the Sorbonne out with her father for a decent meal for once."

He stopped outside a crêperie and made a show of studying the menu. He pulled out his cellphone, checked the screen, and clicked off. He strolled further along the road and made another call.

"All is for go. All is for go. Eight minutes and do what you've got to do. You won't get any other information."

Kaitlyn held her breath as she watched André set a timer on his watch.

"We're going to go in, order a couple of crêpes and then I'm going to go to the toilet. Have you got your gun?"

"I don't want to use it."

"Listen, I don't want you to use it. Believe me if you need to use it, you'll pull it out and fire without a second thought. I'll do the business. If I need cover then do what you need to do, OK?"

"OK."

The place was shabby with Christmas-style electric lamps around a scuffed counter. The benches were plastic and sticky, the tables worn Formica. A balding man of about fifty slouched over and took their order. André selected items from both rucksacks and wandered to the toilet at the far end of the place. She watched the room. Two girl tourists were in the window seat. A thin pale younger guy was turning pancakes on a hot plate. The older man had seated himself at a table and was glancing through a newspaper. Every few seconds he looked up at the door and glanced around the salon. He was trying not to show it, but he was tense. She watched him in a faded mirror on the side wall. Just once he caught her eye. André was ambling back, moving like an elderly man, almost limping. The waiter checked him out and dismissed him as no threat to anyone. André was a class act. He sat down opposite her and did something under the table. He checked his watch, winked at her and took a step toward the seated patron. Without a word he put his hand on the man's head and slammed it down onto the table. The guy gurgled. Kaitlyn watched the young guy doing the pancakes. He reached down behind the counter. She drew the Glock 26.

"Don't even fucking think about it," she said.

The guy froze. André was speaking.

"We've come for Madame Boursellino."

To add emphasis he slammed the guy's head down onto the table once again. "There's a Semtex bomb under the table and a second one in your toilet. Anyone takes me out and there's a guy outside with a phone to fire the detonators."

The younger man had raised his hands. Kaitlyn kept him covered.

"Casse-toi," said the older guy.

"I like you people. You don't have to die. I've left a detonator on that table over there. No bomb, just a tiny detonator. Let me show you."

Suddenly a sheet of flame and a huge *boof* of sound filled the room. André lifted the guy's head by his hair and prepared to drive it face down onto the table again.

"I've come for Signora Boursellino," André repeated.

"OK, OK. In the cellar," said the young man, clearly trembling.

"Show me. Kaitlyn, you're in charge," snapped André.

He came out from behind the counter. Kaitlyn kept the gun on his torso. Head shots were for gangsters and Hollywood. He led André into a corridor behind the counter. Kaitlyn turned her weapon on the patron who was recovering a tooth from the table in front of him. A flimsy door to the side of the room suddenly splintered. Machine gun bullets whined past her head. She opened fire into the smoking doorway. There was a thump and a clatter followed by a silence. Christ, she'd emptied the gun into someone. The two tourist girls in the window seats were screaming as they fled through the door. André burst back into the room carrying a black-haired woman in his arms. He made for the door. Kaitlyn made sure he was out before she backed away.

"The bomb is under this table. Don't fucking move for ten minutes. Don't dream of following me."

She had no idea if any of these people spoke English but her words seemed to do the trick. Once outside she put the gun in her pocket and walked steadily to catch up with André who still had the woman in his arms. They must have hurt her badly. Kaitlyn saw a smile on the older woman's face. The cab driver whom André had spoken to was waiting at the end of the street in La Place du Petit Pont. The door of his Citroen C4 was open.

"Can you believe some bastards would steal a wheelchair?" said André.

"Oh yes, if you don't nail it, they steal it," said the driver. "Once I park up for a pee pee in le Bois de Boulogne and a man steals my wheels."

André laughed as he slid into the back seat with the woman. Kaitlyn took the front passenger seat, turning to look into the intense intelligent eyes of Stella Boursellino. She was truly beautiful, elegant, and strangely kind.

"Do you have injuries?" she asked, falling back on cop instincts and training.

"I'm fine now, as good as ever," came the response in a smoky American voice.

Kaitlyn glanced at this other woman's immobile legs as André still held her.

"Stella never likes anyone to talk about it. She had a riding accident as a child. She can't walk," he said.

Chapter 12

"Let's head for the heliport at Issy-Les-Moulineaux," said André.

He pulled out his cellphone and punched in a number. He didn't seem to get a reply. Kaitlyn watched the tension in his lips and shoulders. She knew. She knew who he was calling. She decided to stay professional. In any event she couldn't talk openly in the taxi. One terrible realization filled her mind. She'd just opened fire into a void and almost certainly killed one or more people. She was involved with guys who used explosives, carried knives and guns, smashed heads into tables without mercy, had infinite wealth and power. A few days ago she'd been a simple London girl, a traffic cop who wanted a home of her own and a man who loved her. Now she was a killer and something like a terrorist. She'd been to bed with one of the richest men in the world and now she was hoping and praying he was still alive as if she was some kind of gangster's moll. Maybe she was just a banker's moll.

The taxi driver had turned up the radio for a news flash in French spoken at the speed of light. He was shaking his head and translating into English.

"Terrorists again, it will never end. They've closed Place Vendôme. There's at least four dead, one witness says there was a grenade and gunfire. Mon Dieu, what is happening in the world?"

Kaitlyn looked back to see the reaction of Stella and André. The woman looked calm, almost serene. André was holding his cellphone to his ear. He shook his head and glanced up. For sure he was calling Randolph. For sure there was no answer.

Their route followed the River Seine. She had no heart to twist her neck to catch the view, except the Eiffel Tower which she had always dreamed of seeing one day. The day was bright, the sky pale, the wind cruelly stripping the last beauty from the trees. Life was flowing along as if nothing had happened. She was a killer. Randolph was dead. She'd lied to her boss. For now she just had to keep it together.

The cab swung onto the open space of what looked like a small airport. A chopper was on the tarmac. It was in the beautiful gray silver livery of Sackman-Platinum Bank.

"No passport controls? No customs?" she said.

"Once a cop always a cop," said André with a laugh.

They scampered to the open door, André carrying Stella as if she were no more than a kitten. He lifted her toward the belly of the aircraft as two strong arms reached out to take her. Kaitlyn's eyes followed them to the shoulders and then to the face. The whine of the jet and the beat of the rotors made conversation impossible. All the same she could shout.

"Randolph, you fucking evil bastard."

In seconds they were climbing away. The Eiffel Tower was just ahead.

"Take a couple of circuits. Kaitlyn's never been to Paris," said Randolph.

This was madness. All the same the beauty of the city took her breath away. The chopper did a slow circle around the tower before putting the nose down and easing across the sky to take in the Arc de Triomphe and the twin towers of the cathedral of Notre Dame.

Randolph took her hand.

"It's wonderful to see you. I had to leave you like that, I hope you'll understand. Just look at this city. Wealth doesn't make you happy, that's true. Wealth only gives you the freedom to be happy or whatever you want to be. One day I'll bring you back here properly, I promise."

This was not the place to talk to him. Where were they going anyway?

It was pointless to talk about the future. How could there be a future when most likely you'll be going to jail for murder unless you stopped a bullet before the police caught up with you?

At least she could see where they were about to land. The pure white sleek perfection of the Demeter Platinum super yacht was beneath them. A minute later they were on the deck as the chopper veered away. Once they'd entered a plush reception area crew members rushed to shake hands and give continental style kisses on both cheeks. A waiter was pouring champagne. She stared at the scene. These folk were rejoicing at death and murder. This was no place for a cop. Randolph had his arm around her shoulders.

"You did a great job," he said.

"Great job? Loosing off a firearm? Assisting in assault and explosives offenses? You're mad and I don't even know what kind of bloody horror you've been involved in."

"Saving a woman from a horrible death, what about that?"

"That was the police's job."

"Exactly, I put a great cop on the job and you saw it through like a pro."

"You're an evil bastard. You didn't put me on any job. You lied to me and you tricked me. Fuck you, Randolph. I never wanted to be a killer."

"Who did you kill?"

"Christ knows. Some thug behind a door with a machine gun."

"Sounds like a nasty character to me. What sort of person behaves like that to a lady?"

"I've got to hand myself in, Randolph. I can't live with the guilt and dread of it all."

"Now you're being that weak little good girl who always wanted to please. Have a drink, take a long hot bath. International banking can get very physical."

"Banking? Fucking banking? What sort of bankers are you?"

"Very rich successful ones. Look, you don't know if you hit anyone. A lot of women couldn't hit a London bus at five yards."

"You are an unbearable patronizing prick sometimes. I'm a good shot."

"You shot a door."

"There was a thump and a clatter."

"You just shot the cat. There's some fucking wild felines in Paris. I bet you no one ever finds a body."

She snatched a glass of champagne. André was proposing a toast to Stella. He was strange brand of chauffeur, for Christ's sake. A crowd had gathered around a big TV which was showing Bloomberg News. A female reporter was speaking from Paris. In the background were armies of police and blue lights. Smoke was rising from a mangled car near some big monument.

"There's concern over the value of the euro against the dollar and other world currency as once again terror strikes at the heart of Paris. Major markets reacted quickly to devalue many European stocks."

Randolph whispered to Stella who had appeared in a wheelchair.

"It's OK, we covered our positions before we went in. We're set to buy back and take profits as soon as the panic dies down. Should be about twenty million dollars for a day's work."

"I'll treasure it, Randolph. All in all I'd rather have just had a night's sleep at the Ritz," said Stella with a wry smile on her wide sensual lips.

The reporter continued.

"Police sources are saying that a grenade exploded in a Mercedes limo containing four men. A number of firearms were found in the wreckage of the vehicle. The theory is that the explosion took place as they were on their way to commit an act of terror. So far the dead have not been identified. The French government have said there is no need to lose confidence in Paris as a financial center. The European Central Bank will pump in whatever is needed if markets fall."

"Yeah, go for it," said Randolph with a smug chuckle. "We'll spoon up that gravy all day. Might make thirty million, Stella."

"What? Is that all you care about?" asked Kaitlyn.

"Look, terror and war can be good business if you're on your toes and know the right side of the deal. Don't bother your head with it."

"Right now I'd rather jump in the ocean than bother with you."

"Grab another glass of champagne then come and relax for a while. It's going to be a late lunch, early dinner by the look of the time."

He didn't care. He simply did *not* fucking well care. She was on a ship somewhere in the middle of a sea. There weren't too many places to go. She grabbed a glass, took an unladylike swig and grabbed another. OK, she was going to the dogs and she sure wouldn't get champagne in jail.

She slumped down on one of the leather sofas in Randolph's suite. He seated himself in a chair to face her. His eyes were still kind and had a look. A look she could only describe as loving. Her education in psychology was ringing a bell louder and louder in her head. This guy was a psychopath. The charm, the lack of human feeling, the lack of fear or conscience.

"Kaitlyn, thanks for what you did. There was no other way Stella was going to get free."

She didn't answer, didn't pull her eyes away from his. He was gorgeous, fearless and so much stronger than her. She hated men like this. How she hated this man for what he could make her feel and want. She was still a cop and a cop asks questions.

"What happened in Paris with that car?"

"I had a rendezvous. Some gentlemen wanted to meet me alone in Place Vendôme, a very public open space. Nowhere to hide, no way to have hidden assistants like a magician. The car pulled up and some silly boy had his bullet proof window open to point a gun at me. These thugs are amateurs. I popped in a little present they weren't expecting."

"And then?"

"I ran like Mick the Miller."

"Who?"

"Mick the Miller, the most famous greyhound of all time. He's in the American hall of fame."

"You're a psycho. You're talking as if you don't care, like it's almost a joke."

"I can understand you seeing it that way. These guys have no mercy, no heart, no faith, no conscience. It's true I've spent too long around them. Sometimes I just want out. To be honest I look at you and I know I'm going to build a better life one day. In the meantime I'm as mean as these crooks because that's the way I stay alive. It won't always be that way."

"I want to believe you and I hate myself for that because deep down I know you're bad. I can't believe you can make love so sensitively, so lovingly and then get out of bed and murder four guys."

"Self-defense, officer. That's a legit plea in all the courts of the world."

She shook her head. He could always turn everything around and make it seem normal and decent. She asked another cop question.

"So how could you have known there'd be an open window. How did you know the explosion wouldn't kill you?"

"These guys always smoke, there's always an open window. Let me explain something important. Nothing works the way you want all the time. An armored limo will keep out bullets and bombs. That's brilliant because they also keep them in. Always remember that little bit of schoolboy physics, my dear. Very little blast came out."

The champagne was hitting her brain hard. She laid her head back. She'd forgotten something. Something big.

"Fuck! There's still two Semtex bombs in that café place in Paris."

Randolph smiled.

"It's always nice to leave a tip. When they get bored and take a close look they'll be able to use it on a pancake."

"Semtex plastic explosive?"

"Marzipan with an old torch battery sticking out. André had one detonator, that's all. The rest was a bluff. Did you believe there was a third guy outside ready to destroy the place?"

"I didn't think. André spoke mainly French."

She had to hand it to these bastards. They were cool and brave beyond all human reason. Where could she go next in her life? Her cellphone was ringing. She pulled it from the pocket of her hoodie. Maybe she'd soon know her direction. It was DCI Shannon Knightsmith.

Chapter 13

"Where's that bastard, Quinn?" said Shannon at once.

"Hi, he's right here. I'm looking at him."

"There's mayhem in Paris. There's bombs in a café in the Latin Quarter. There's four dead in Place de Vendôme. The French police are going crazy. Their president's been on the phone to the prime minister."

"Was Randolph involved?"

"He must have been. Get to somewhere we can talk."

She glanced across at Randolph. The phone was loud enough for him to hear. He put his finger to his lips then pressed his hands together as if in prayer. His eyes were pleading.

"It's OK. He's gone."

He blew her a kiss with a warm smile. She was mad, plain fucking mad.

"We don't know if he was involved but I know it in my bones. We followed a transponder trace of a Sackman-Platinum helicopter around Paris. In air space like that you get shot down if you piss them off, so they had to keep their tracker on for air traffic control. It took off from Paris heliport at Issy then did some fucking stupid sightseeing stuff around the town."

"Would anyone do that if they were involved in all that shit?"

Randolph was beaming and applauding. Kaitlyn could hear Shannon breathing as if in thought.

"That's a good point but these guys aren't normal. Anyway, once they were out of Paris air space they did the MH370 trick and turned off all their systems. Have any choppers landed on that Queen Mary-style yacht?"

Kaitlyn had very little time to think.

"I don't think so, but this thing is huge and I might not see it."

"And Randolph Quinn, where's he been all day."

Too late to turn back, Kaitlyn. Too late!

"As far as I know in his office or somewhere around me. Since the Ritz shooting he's been buying and selling currencies to cash in on the markets."

"They're fucking parasites, feeding off misery. Look, this is the bottom line. Those hoods killed in Paris were actually under observation. They're known suppliers of arms to terror groups. The president is not happy that some monkey popped a hand grenade through the window of their car but no one is worried that they're dead. Let's just say they're not wasting a lot of time looking for the people who did it. This stuff hits the tourist business."

"Is everything about money?"

"Yes."

"What about CCTV from Paris?"

"Sure, they've got some great shots of a guy coming out of a shop wearing a rubber Donald Trump mask. The target car was circling the square. We don't know why. The killer wandered out, head down, collar up, did the business and wandered off still wearing his mask."

"What do you want me to do?" asked Kaitlyn.

"I know this must be horrible for you. You're not trained for this kind of thing. Hang in there and note everything. Are you OK with this?"

"I'm OK, yeah, I'm good."

"Good girl. Keep your phone charged."

She let out a long sigh. She wanted to cry. Why had she lied and lied again? Maybe she didn't want to tell her boss that a Metropolitan Police officer had been running around Paris, been in a shootout and had been sleeping with the guy who'd just done four murders.

He was kneeling in front of her holding both her hands. She looked down at her knees, not wanting to meet his eyes. She didn't have to respond to him. Not if she didn't want to.

"My lovely woman, my dear lovely friend. This is hell for you, isn't it? How can I thank you?"

"Leave me alone, get me a vodka and a cigarette," she said feeling the pull of his gaze on her.

"Cigarette?"

"That's what they give to the condemned guy in all the movies. This may as well be a film for all I know of reality. The one way you can thank me is to open up and do what

Scotland Yard want. Give evidence against these people, accept witness protection. Maybe you're the richest man in the world but no one can live like this. I've got enough on you to get you locked up for life."

"See, I knew I was right to trust you."

"So why do you trust me? I'm a nobody. I'm a traffic cop who just happened to turn up at your crash."

"And, you're pretty gorgeous, you're brave, you're not on the take, you're not a gold digger and, and, well maybe I felt something special for you."

His hand stroked her cheek. She pressed it against her face.

"Randolph, I'm afraid. I don't want to go to jail. I don't want to die. I want to get drunk and sing karaoke with some girlfriends."

"But you want to stay with me, don't you?"

She had to look up and find his eyes.

"Yes. Yes I do and you're going to ruin my life and throw me away sometime between now and when you die. I don't think either of us have too long to wait."

"No time to lose then," he replied as his lips brushed hers. How could she be aroused after all that had happened? How could she be clutching his head, holding him in the kiss? How could her body be opening to him, needing his touch? His hand gently massaged her breast, she was reaching behind herself to undo her bra, feeling the soft release of her breasts, feeling his lips at her nipple. That jolt went to her clitoris pushing her little shaft hard against the crotch of her jeans. How could she? How could she go for this in a room where anyone could walk in, where anyone could be watching? He was standing, undoing his fly. His cock was big and hard. How could she be pulling off her jeans, just throwing aside her panties, brushing her own wetness, feeling the spasm of her body as his tongue found her groove, leaving her convulsing? His hot cock filled the void, stroked her magic spot, pulsed its own need and lust deep and deeper into her, filling her mind with his bass groan, adding her own cry of ecstasy as waves of back-arching orgasm rippled through her belly. She thought of his dick, jetting out his seed as he was coming into her pulsing flesh. His lips on hers, still wet with her own sex juice, kissed her through her aftershocks of pure animal passion. God, what had she become? What?

"You're the most wonderful woman," he said in his deep voice. His eyes were misty, unfocused yet filled with that dark, rich, kindness that lay beneath all his bullshit and arrogance.

"And you, Randolph, are a sexy man. One day I'll hate myself for this."

"But not today, not tonight?"

"No, not tonight, you bastard."

Chapter 14

He held her hand as they stood on the promenade deck. The sea was smooth, inky black reflecting the light of the full moon. Still she buzzed with the joy of their lovemaking. The heat and essence of him was still in the hot core of her sexual being. He was gorgeous and made her feel beautiful and desired. She'd always suspected that one day she'd sell her soul for the right man. So far she'd just rolled over and given it away; to the *wrong* man.

"Where are we?"

"You're in my thoughts, and my heart," he said.

"Fuck you, don't play with me."

He turned her to him.

"That's not kind. I was being honest."

"You were being tricky, talking about your heart but not showing any feeling, like I could be in your liver or in your kidneys."

"You're in all those places too. You could be a whole meat pie for a man. I mean ... I don't know, Kaitlyn, you're right. It was a tricky trite line. I won't say anything like that again."

"Fuck you. I want you to talk about things, want you to want me."

She shut up. She was digging a hole.

"We're off the coast of Portugal, heading south toward the Straits of Gibraltar and the Mediterranean."

"That sounds so romantic. You know in your arms I could dream of a future, knowing now that I can feel up to some kind of limit I didn't even know was there. Maybe beyond all limits, not that I'd be with you, of course. Then I remember that I'm a criminal and a killer and that I'm not a police officer. That I'm not fit to call myself such a thing."

He leaned back against the rail and looked at her with a confident seriousness she hadn't seen in him before. She had to watch his face.

"When all this began I asked you to trust me. I can justify that and one day you will know how and why. That was a day at the office. Here, tonight on this ocean I'm asking you to trust me as a man, as your lover. You deserve to know that I love you Kaitlyn and that I'm in your hands in more ways than you can imagine."

"You love me? You dump me out of helicopter with a gun and some commando guy I don't know and you fuck off into the skies without a word. Is that what a girl gets out of love?"

"Well, what did you want? A diamond ring? I'm a poor guy. I've got to save up."

"You couldn't afford me."

"I know that, so don't ask me to give up the day job just yet."

"You're a jerk."

"You hungry?"

"Yup."

This time it was lobster, succulent exotic lobster. She couldn't deny the thrill of being in this luxury with a man who had eyes only for her, who had at least said he loved her. Of course it was bullshit, just a throwaway to keep her on side. All the same he'd said it and she'd chucked it back in his handsome face. Who the fuck did this guy think he was?

It was warm enough to sit on the deck, nursing a generous measure of cognac in crystal balloon glasses. The vessel plowed on through a gentle swell. She was aware of her woman sex, gently aroused as she thought of his helpless desire for her. She tightened her pelvic muscles a little to tease out ripples of pleasure as she watched his lips on the glass, thought of his abandoned groans and flood of man juice into her sucking belly. She'd had this man and he longed for her. Had said he loved her. Maybe *really* loved her. Now the world's smoothest finest brandy was talking in her ear. *Just shut the fuck up, Kaitlyn.* This gorgeous guy craves to kiss the joy from her hot sex, show his power by making her lose it, come against his lips. *Pour another brandy. Let Ishtar speak for her. Let it be. Let it be.*

He slept spooned into her back, his lips occasionally pressing butterfly kisses onto her neck and shoulders. Now and then the scene at the café, the splintering door, the machine gun bullets and her return of fire replayed in her mind. She could never hope to get away with this, yet his arm was around her, his sleep serene. She was safe and she had only defended herself after all. She was protected by a fearless man who had the world by the scruff of the neck. *A man for whom she felt, well let's not go there, Kaitlyn.*

She dressed in her room. Her H&M clothes seemed out of place here, but she was a middle-class girl and her rent took more than half her wages. The ten-year-old Nissan 350Z was still on finance, she still had a few thousand dollars of student debt. In Randolph's world a day at the office yesterday had netted something like thirty million dollars. She shrugged, recalling how her father had always joked she was sure of a rich husband with her good looks.

She chose some black calf-length leggings with frilly bottoms and a light half-sleeved white top. She added her sparkly flip-flop sandals. *Well, Kaitlyn you're a cheap and cheerful girl, so there you go.* There was a knock at the door. Randolph didn't knock doors. He paid guys to knock doors that need knocking; but most doors just opened.

"Yo."

"Yo to you too," said the smoky American voice of Stella Boursellino as she swept into the room in a wheelchair. She leaned forward and made a gesture with her lips, signaling Kaitlyn to perform the continental cheek kissing. Bloody hell, this woman was beautiful, or at least beautifully presented. Raven hair that shone like a dark marble, wide almond-shaped deep, almost maroon eyes set in perfect pure whites, sensual full lips with a smile or a kiss playing with the choices as she spoke in her deep sultry voice. Her makeup was perfect, her hands manicured and carrying a couple of diamond rings to die for. Kaitlyn kept her eyes on the beauty of this woman, not looking at her immobile legs dressed in deep blue leather pants.

"I had business yesterday with all the market turmoil. Randolph promised me maybe thirty million, but he had a beautiful girl on his mind. I squeezed out another million or two with a few taps on my laptop."

"Lucky Randolph. Who was the girl?" asked Kaitlyn. Was this woman having a poke at her for distracting him from the normal process of greed?

Stella laughed and reached out a hand. Kaitlyn responded by offering her own. Her touch was strong and warm.

"I'm sorry. I wasn't complaining. It's hard to compliment another woman on her beauty. Well, it's hard for me because I'm a vain bitch."

Kaitlyn had to smile. Stella Boursellino seemed like her type of woman.

"You've every right to be vain. I'll take a rain check on the bitch since I don't know you yet."

"All vanity is a capricious bitch believe me. If you're a follower of Ishtar you'll know that."

Stella's eyes were on the tattoo.

"You know of her?"

"Studied mythology at college, but that's not why I came. You guys saved my life yesterday. Those bastards threw me in that cellar and even if Randolph had handed himself over they'd have put a bullet in my head."

"André is one hell of a guy."

"How was he? Was he emotional?"

"Emotional? No, calm and professional."

"Did he talk about me?"

"He said you were beautiful."

"That's better, maybe I'll let him off a little if he said that. I'd have expected a bit of passion," said Stella with a rich laugh.

Kaitlyn raised her eyebrows. What was she saying?

"My dear, André is my man, my lover, my husband."

Oh my God, she'd said some spiteful jealous things to André and he hadn't given her any clue that he was Stella's husband. Maybe he'd had the sense of diplomacy to keep it to himself. Her mind fired back to the way he had held her, carried her away from almost certain death without a thought for himself or indeed for Kaitlyn herself. Stella seemed to pick up on her stunned expression.

"I bet Randolph didn't tell you because he's a bastard. He likes to hint and tease he's been my lover. I like that too, and for a woman, a woman in a wheelchair, you've no idea how that makes me feel. He does it as a little parcel of joy that's so beautifully wrapped that no one can ever open it. I know it and he knows it. He's a bastard, but a bastard with a big heart."

Kaitlyn sat down. These guys had complex lives and relationships. She loved the openness of this woman.

"André?" she began.

"Right, I think I can anticipate your questions. My body is in this chair but believe me I am not. The heavens were merciful to me when I had my accident. I can function fully as a woman with all those pains and pleasures. I have a chateau in France and I met André one evening. We talked about vines and wine. We have been together ever since. He has no greed, no arrogance and no jealousy. He drives an old van and spends a day breaking open walnuts. If he touches the soil a plant grows up."

"He acted like a commando."

"That's because he was. He was a special services soldier and went on to work as a presidential guard. He's one hell of a guy."

"So Randolph came to you for a job?"

"Yeah. He was a cocky little cockney street kid with a missing front tooth. He'd lost it in a fight the night before the interview. He's like a terrier with money. He sniffs it out and won't let go."

Kaitlyn sighed. There was just so much she wanted to know about Sackman-Platinum Bank and Randolph himself. Why did trivia always interest her so much?

"He'd lost a tooth?"

"Yeah, the bank had it fixed. He's bionic like part titanium and ceramic."

Kaitlyn laughed.

"So he can lose a fight?"

"We never saw the other guy. Put it this way, he has made us some of the very richest people in the world and we don't lose many trades."

Here's your chance; Kaitlyn. You're still on the books as a cop and maybe you can redeem something before you go to jail.

"But you get involved with some pretty nasty people, like the kind of people we met yesterday?"

Stella Boursellino fixed her with a stare.

"You're a woman but you're also a cop. An international bank deals with the whole world, whatever that world is. We have to respect the confidentiality of our clients."

"You mean 'Fuck off and keep your snout out of our money laundering business.'"

"I mean that many rich powerful people are risk-taking dominant individuals."

"Crooks, traffickers of drugs and people, pimps, robbers, waste dumpers, sweat shop slave-drivers, arms dealers, and maybe other shit I can't even imagine."

"Cops would see the world in this way. Kaitlyn, I can never forget that you helped to save my life. I know you have shown support and loyalty to Randolph, and I respect that. There are things I'm bursting to tell you. I'm longing to tell you but I cannot. I *cannot*."

"What could you possibly tell me that would make any difference? A bunch of murderers are at war with you guys either because you've ripped them off or they just want more of the cake. The Metropolitan Police are offering protection in exchange for evidence. I'm sure we'll stretch that to cover you too."

"It's a kind offer. A woman in a wheelchair is harder to hide. Your police offered Randolph a safe house and they petrol bombed it. I suspect I would have died, don't you? It was interesting to test how good you guys are."

Kaitlyn sighed. Stella was right. Too bloody right. So, Randolph had agreed to play along as an experiment. Her reply was lame and without conviction.

"The offer is always there."

"Before I go, please listen carefully to what I say. Randolph wants you at his side. You've no idea how many girls pop up to seduce the handsome and richest man in the world. You've no idea how much you are a gift of beauty and innocence to him. He's a loving man who can trust no girl. He'll never tell you but he's had some sorrow in his life and not a lot of love. Someone like you could attract any man. You showed him kindness and you showed him your honest courage and I believe you have shown him your passion and joy as a woman. He won't tell you these things so directly. Normally it wouldn't be my place to tell you, but think of this as war time when all the normal constraints are set aside."

She studied the older woman's face. She liked her, respected her but how could she trust her?

"You know I've kind of burned my bridges already. I don't know why I should tell you this but I care about him. We clicked right from the first glance. Can things ever really be like that, like in some magazine story?"

"Why yes, but I would never have said that before I met André. Love is a brutal education, it can't make you smarter but it can beat your ignorance to death. Ishtar herself would have told you that."

"So, Stella, I've no idea why I'm asking you this but where the fuck do I go from here?"

"You're asking me because I'm here and you need an answer. Keep your nerve and stick with it. You won't regret it in the end. You're the good guys but the fact is you don't have the strength or the resources to deal with these people."

"How can crooks be so strong?"

"The world has changed. Governments chop away financial regulations and starve agencies like police. The Internet concentrates power and allows criminals to infiltrate every portion of every life. We're struggling against the greatest enemy that freedom and integrity have ever faced. And it comes into your life like a friend. Sackman-Platinum feeds off them, it's true. We have no choice. We have no choice."

"Maybe I won't bother with another smart-phone."

Stella reached out her hand once again. Kaitlyn took it and closed it with her other hand.

"I'm not advising you to do something I didn't do myself. Trust him. That's my last word," said Stella, spinning her chair around and heading for the door.

Chapter 15

She sat down, inwardly shaking her head. How could she just leap into a relationship with a man who'd already wrecked her career and maybe her whole life? She needed a friend. She brought up Camille's number. For sure they would monitor her call but all she wanted was a chat.

"Camille?"

"Bloody hell, bloody fucking hell. Where are you? Where have you been? I was scooped up yesterday afternoon by a team from the National Crime Agency, Interpol and some DCI called Shannon out of Scotland Yard. They take me to a meet with some guys who I know were spooks, like MI5 and CIA."

"What? What did they want to know?"

"Stuff like if you were on the level? Did you have boyfriends? Did you have spotted or striped panties or eat vegan sausages? Mainly they wanted to know what the fuck you were up to in a shootout with super-crooks in Paris?"

"Paris?"

"Yeah, Paris, like you didn't know. Facial recognition cameras picked you up at the rail station Gare du Nord and some other place I can't remember. Some military colonel from European Intelligence wanted to know if you liked marzipan like it was some sort of in joke I didn't get."

Kaitlyn got it. She got it. When had DCI Shannon Knightsmith known? She pushed her worries aside.

"Can you check out Sackman-Platinum Bank? I want to know everything about them."

"Hang on girl, that stuff's not your brief. Just what are you up to?"

"I can't tell you because I don't know. Randolph Quinn just possibly could have the key to world crime. I just don't know."

"No one's going to thank you for solving world crime."

"It'd look good on my CV," she said, amazed she'd been so flippant.

"Have you been on some skunk or something?"

"I wish."

"Kaitlyn, get a grip. I know your need for a man, I know that itch you can't reach, hun, but this guy, this guy is a hood in a suit. He's going to die, splattered against a wall or strangled and thrown in a sewer."

"You don't know the situation I'm in here. I can't just walk away."

"Quinn won't kill a cop. The politics are too difficult."

"Well, thanks for the vote of confidence. Maybe he likes me."

"You're sleeping with him aren't you, or at least sharing a bed. You'll chase your hot little pussy across a road and you'll get crushed."

Kaitlyn sighed. Camille had a talent for words.

"Two things. What time did those guys scoop you up?"

"Just after 2 p.m. What's the other thing?"

"Check out Sackman-Platinum. Balance sheets, names of directors, addresses of offices, credit ratings. You're the detective, just anything and everything."

"You know they'll be on this call at GCHQ and probably half the intelligence agencies of the world. I've been told to report any contact with you. I have no choice."

"People keep telling me that. I understand and it doesn't matter. I'm sticking with this and trusting my instincts and my luck."

"Ciao, baby. Get your ass out of there. Love you."

"Love you."

OK, let's work this out. The shootout was at about midday French time. Some team of powerful types had grabbed Camille just a little while after and DCI Knightsmith had called her after they'd gotten back on the ship. Simple, Shannon had known she'd been in Paris, had already been at the meeting with Camille and those other guys. She knew she'd been lying but she'd just played it along like it was a girlie chat. So what did Shannon know and whose side was she on? *Kaitlyn, have you been set up by guys playing a longer game than you can imagine?* One thing was for certain. She couldn't trust her boss but did someone want her to know that? Camille must have already been on their radar and they must have guessed she'd be in touch with her friend. If the phone lying on her bed were to ring, would she answer it? The one person who could help her was a guy who'd killed four men with a hand grenade in broad daylight in the middle of Paris, her gorgeous lover and the richest man in the world. What did she have to lose?

She wanted to call her mother but something stopped her. If these Silicon Alley crooks had geeky tentacles in every nook and cranny of existence, maybe somehow they could trace the call, at least to an area. They could use private facial recognition CCTV from something like a shopping center or even subvert the police system to find her. OK. Her university course had covered paranoia. Stuff like that didn't happen. She picked up her cellphone, switched it off, and pulled out the battery. God, she was a long way from home.

An alarm was sounding, like some kind of emergency. Randolph strode in.

"Come with me, we've got a little situation up on deck. You'll be safe. She followed him up a clanging stairwell to a bare room with small slits filled with bullet proof glass for windows. She peered out. A team of sailors, some with weapons resembling long pipes were dressed in full military gear on the deck just below.

"What's going on?"

"It's a rogue aircraft. These thugs have many light planes for their drug- and people-smuggling operations. A local guy wants to impress the bosses so he's buzzing us for a bit of fun, just to let us know they know where we are. He'll send back a couple of pictures to show what a tough guy he is. A lot of thugs do what they do for the status just as much as for the money."

"So what's with the military stuff out there?"

"He wants to show off and so do we. The weapons are FIM92s. You probably know them as Stingers."

"This is crazy Randolph. Will they open fire?"

"That's not my decision. Captain Fuller directs operations. I'm a passenger like you."

"It's a weird kind of cruise."

"Yeah, I keep telling Stella we should push out a few brochures."

Without warning a missile flared and streaked into the air. She followed it to a point where a small aircraft hung in the sky. A large spinning chunk spiraled down in flames into the sea.

"Guess that spoiled his day," said Randolph.

"Don't tell me that was marzipan. It's murder."

"You could say that. It shouldn't have surprised him since he's in the murder business."

"You knew who it was?"

"Sure, Shaban Pisha; he's an Albanian Mafia killer and trafficker of teenage prostitutes mainly into London. He just loves his Portuguese estate. He runs a little refugee trafficking business from here for pocket money and he likes to throw his weight around. He just flew out to frighten us with his ugly mug. Now his bosses will know not to bother us."

"Randolph we do need to talk. I really, really need some answers."

"I'm an open book. First get your case packed. In about two hours we're going ashore."

"I can't see any land."

"We're too far out. The ship won't change course so we'll be using a fast launch. Just think of the Portuguese cozido I'm going to get you."

"Cozido?"

"It's a fabulous stew made with a bunch of stuff."

"Sounds like my life story."

"Then we'll talk. Promise."

Chapter 16

She began to pack mechanically, as if she no longer had any personal being. She was no more than a cork in an ocean of events, of killing, of warfare. She took a deep breath almost as if trying to stay afloat. What could she cling to? Stella had told her to trust him. Camille had told her to get out at all costs. She could no longer trust the police or even her boss. She was alone and she had nothing but her own judgment. She had time for a shower. The sensation of the water seemed to block her thoughts and cares. She was a creature like any other in the flow of time. She let the water tease her along the edge of her sex, letting the sensation take away her mind, focusing on that tension building as she let her hand caress between her legs. She couldn't do this. How could she do this? How could she? She'd closed her eyes, hands were on her breasts, a man's hands.

"Randolph, what the fuck?"

He must have come in from his suite, must have seen what she was doing. He was naked, hard, and like a warm soothing rock behind her.

"Don't stop for me," came his deep voice

He parted her legs, sliding into her from behind, filling her being with his strength and lust for her. She felt held and opened, helpless and beyond restraint. Her own hand brought her to the peak as his hot cock stroked the sweet spot inside her. She grunted out a surge of sound, unbound of all modesty. It was a cry of pure nature, wild and shameless.

("Fuck my pussy, fucking come in me."

She threw her head back as his lips and teeth found her neck and shoulders. His hand was on her clitoris, his unstoppable shaft driving urgently the length of her flesh. She was coming again. His drive was endless; she could hold and build, certain of his muscular power. She was groaning, just holding herself at that delicious pinnacle.

"Come. Fucking let go. Come on my dick, my sweet lover," he growled against her cheek as he held her belly with the flat on his hand, thrusting his pouring cock to her limits.

Her orgasm burst in her own rush of sound. She convulsed forward, her legs losing strength, confident of his grip. He held her like a sighing rag doll, lost in the massive force of her own release and the resolving waves of his ejaculation. God, she had never come like that. Never, never so wanton, so absolutely out of her mind. He turned her to him, raised her chin and kissed her lips with a tenderness so much in contrast with his iron sexual force. His eyes questioned hers, almost pleading for a response. If he was trying to look into her, she was looking back with the same desire. They had known each other as creatures, abandoned to the lust and spill of nature. Now, in this moment of their souls, they were meeting as beings of emotion and need.

"I love you," he said.

No, no no, he couldn't say that, not after this short time. He couldn't say that when she had no balanced picture of her life or position. She shook her head.

"Don't you want me to love you?"

"Yes, you know I would."

"Would?"

"Would if you weren't some kind of psychopathic killer billionaire."

He smiled.

"Hey, that would look cool on my business cards."

"Randolph. None of this is real. I do care about you. I want. I want. I want to look at our relationship away from luxury yachts, away from guns, missiles, champagne, murder, the fear of death and prison."

He smiled.

"I think I'll take that as a yes then," he said kissing her forehead. "We'll be away from the ship in ten minutes. You see, I'm already solving all your issues."

"Well, thanks," she said, unable to stop returning his smile. The guy was impossible.

A sleek gray boat with the lines of a whale was waiting in the hangar. Two sailors were already aboard. Randolph helped her into a waterproof hooded jacket, strapped her in, and took his seat beside her.

"What sort of boat is this?" she asked.

"It's an M46 Interceptor, one of the fastest in the world. Hold on."

The outer door slid aside. A cold swirling wind swept in. The boat roared and powered out into a dusky evening of white-topped waves. They bounced and flew through a wild sea. She clung on, begging for the ride to end before she was sick. Slowly shoreline lights grew brighter ahead of them in the gathering darkness. She could make out the red and green lamps of a harbor entrance.

"Is that where we're going?" she yelled.

"Harbors are for tourists. We're going to hit the beach."

"I'm not a marine."

"Everyone's got to start somewhere. Can you swim?"

"No."

"That's a lie."

He was right. The boat cut the motor and nudged up to a long sandy beach. An open Jeep Cherokee was waiting but no driver was in sight. Randolph leaped out into shallow water and reached for her, swinging her clear onto the sand. He grabbed their luggage as the craft roared back into life and disappeared without marker lamps into the darkness. He led the way to the Jeep, reached underneath to retrieve a key and started the motor. She scrambled in.

"Where are we?"

"South coast of Portugal, the Algarve, a place called Vale do Lobo. I've got a little place here and we happened to be passing. Stella's going to cruise round to Venice. She needs a break and she can work from the ship."

"And the bad guys, or should I say the marginally worse guys, think you're still on board?"

"I'd like to think that, but satellites have high resolution cameras and often infra red sensors. They'll be watching."

"How the fuck can you live like this?"

"Baby, we all live like this. It's just that most people are too poor to be worth finding."

"You're a complete heartless cynic."

"Not complete, but I'm working on it," he replied without rancor, engaging drive and setting off across the sand.

They made a tour of a small town. She noted his attention to his mirrors. He did a couple of U-turns. He knew how to beat obvious surveillance. They pulled up at the gates of a huge house, more like a futuristic palace in plate glass and white. Powerful floodlights snapped on. Randolph entered a number into his phone and waited as the gates swung open. Two armed men inside raised their hands in greeting as they drove in.

"Those guys are carrying assault rifles," she said.

"We get a lot of trouble with squirrels."

"Fuck off. What is this?"

He turned to her sharply.

"Listen, this is how it has to be. We'll eat and I'll explain as much as I can. There's guards and surveillance all around this place. Don't wander off 'cause there's electric fences, attack dogs, and snake pits."

"Jesus."

"OK. I exaggerated about the snakes."

"I feel better now."

They drove straight into a large garage, a heavy shutter closing down behind them. They walked through into a spacious modern kitchen.

"Home sweet home, honey. How'd you like to play Mrs Quinn?"

"What?"

"I gave everyone the night off. Let's cook. I'm happy to play Mr Quinn."

"You're a nightmare," she sighed. "What are we cooking?"

"Cozido, I told you already." He went to a cavernous fridge and took out a variety of vegetables. "Shred the cabbage and peel the stuff like turnips and carrots. I'll do the meat."

While she worked he took out some beef and some dark-looking sausage. From the window she could see lawns and an infinity swimming pool.

"Who owns this place, the bank?"

"No, it's mine, but we all use it for business."

"It's a palace."

"Nah, I've got a real palace in Montenegro. I'd sell you this place for twenty million dollars."

"Christ, it would take you all morning to make that."

"Yeah, business has been a bit slow, but not that bad. If I got up late and had an early lunch it would be about that figure."

"You make me sick."

83

"Why?"

"The greed, the arrogance."

"Thank God you didn't mean my cooking. Now *that* I would have taken personally."

She looked up from her vegetables.

"Don't mock a woman holding a chef's knife."

He glanced back at the point of the knife in her hand wagging in his direction. He knew he'd pushed it a bit too far. She liked him to know the boundaries.

"Right, that'll take a couple of hours. Let's go downstairs," he announced.

She shrugged and followed him through luxurious lounges, a games room with snooker tables, a Jacuzzi, a cinema, and a gym. At last they arrived in a wide atrium with a white marble floor and pillars. In the corner was an ugly steel door which looked like a safe. He spun the central wheel and punched in four separate codes on four separate panels which dropped down from the wall. Finally he turned the wheel again a number of times in either direction. This was serious shit. The door was heavy, at least bomb-proof. He motioned for her to follow him down a plain concrete stairwell until they arrived at another armored door with more codes. As she walked in she was struck by the warm electric air and the buzz of computer terminals and overhead screens showing the stock markets of the world. Operators worked calmly, monitors flicked from white to red to green. A device like a clock flashed high on the wall, pulsing out impossibly long numbers.

"What's that thing?" she asked.

"It's just a party trick. The guys work in four, six-hour shifts. We reset the display for each team. They like to beat the other guys. They can glance up and see what they've made."

"Made?"

"Yeah. We're trading the Far and Mid East tonight. These guys have clocked up seventeen million dollars. I'll speak to their team leader to see if he can shake them up a bit."

"We didn't cook for this number of guests."

"They're self-contained. They eat and sleep here."

"What sort of life is that?"

"It's the dream baby. They don't do it forever. It's wealth. *Wealth*."

"Randolph, you make millions every minute it seems. The hoods want some slice of the cake or some cash they believe you've stolen. Why don't you just cut them in and move on?"

"What? Me? Give in to crooks?"

She shook her head. These people lived in a different world.

"We can communicate safely from here. All our trades and communications use an encrypted laser system. We don't use cables, satellites, the Internet, flags or pigeons. I'd actually put more faith in the security of a pigeon than the Internet. We trade faster than any other operation in the world. The world plays the markets. We *work* the markets."

A cheer went up from a couple of operators who stood and did high-fives. The counter ripped on to twenty-three million. *Wealth*. She watched while Randolph went to a terminal and put on a headset. He reached for an old-fashioned pencil and notepad. He spoke quickly in single words, scribbling down what looked like phone numbers, names, and addresses. He tore off the sheet and pushed it into the back pocket of his jeans. He stood and turned back to her without explanation.

"I wanted you to see the show. Believe me, one day it'll all make more sense. I'm starving."

They ate in the kitchen, Randolph serving her the cozido with some plain rice. She had to admit it was delicious. It was lovely for these few minutes to be just folk in a kitchen eating a family style meal. The thought saddened and for a moment overwhelmed her. Tears ran down her cheeks.

"Maybe we could have been people like this if we weren't killers and criminals."

He took her hand.

"We can still be whatever we want, trust me. We're just flying through a bit of turbulence."

"Maybe so and you're going to crash. What good is it for me to bother caring about you?"

"Because, because things aren't always exactly what they seem. Tell me; what do you think of crooks. I mean bad, bad criminals?"

"I'm a cop, I loathe them."

"So do I. So do André and Stella. So do all those guys downstairs. So does your mother."

"But you do business with them. You trade using their money and skim the profits."

"Kaitlyn, one dollar bill looks just like another. We don't always know how a client gets his money."

"That's PR bullshit for a schmuck jury and you know it."

"Just think of it this way. Sure Sackman-Platinum gets rich but those hoods are just a little bit poorer than they would be."

"So it's OK if you hit them with a hand grenade, shoot them down with a Stinger missile?"

"It's expedient."

"It's me or them, or it used to be."

"Used to be?"

"Sure, now it's you and me or them."

"You're mad."

"Yes, and you've got proof"

"What proof?"

"I love you. That's just too fucking crazy for words."

He was smiling as if there was nothing in the world but her and some dishes to wash. She wanted to kiss his arrogant mouth. She closed her eyes as he drew her to him, protected her, loved her, or at least had the feel of love.

"If you love me, get me through this. One simple task and I'll love you Randolph Quinn and that's a real promise of love."

"We're coming through this, Kaitlyn. And now I've got a real reason."

"You're full of fake shit."

"Fake shit smells better than real shit."

"This conversation is going downhill. OK, what are we doing here and where are we going?"

"We're here for tonight and maybe for a while tomorrow. Then it looks like Milan. We'll pop over there and get you a couple of frocks. Now what do you say?"

"Milan, just like that?"

"Just like Sackman-Platinum private jet."

"Window seat?"

"Yeah."

"What's the real reason for going?"

"There's a guy there, someone who could make peace with us."

"Promise?"

"Promise."

"Deal."

She awoke into the stillness at 3 a.m. Without the noise and action of the day the terror of her situation gripped her. She'd agreed to fly to Milan out of bravado. No way was she letting him know her fear. Now she was off the ship she could escape, run to a police station maybe? As a simple cop there'd always been some sort of back up, some supervisor to give her an order. She was so far out of her depth, she might as well just give up and sink. Should she call DCI Shannon Knightsmith, admit she'd been lying and confront her with what she knew? Should she stick with him and still try to get all the inside story she could on these crooks? And here she was in bed with this man, completely compromised sexually and emotionally. She knew why. He was so gorgeous and she wanted him. Some things in her character would never change. Had she ever thought that the tattoo of an all powerful goddess could transform her? At heart she'd always wanted to be the good girl, own up to guilt, get the top marks, make her mother proud, sing karaoke rather than join a band. If she saw her chance she'd make a run for it and forget him. He had no right to stop her. Maybe. He stirred, wrapped his arm around her, kissed her shoulder. Maybe not.

Too soon the day was squeezing through the long vertical blinds of the room. Randolph pushed a button at his bedside to open them. The view that filled the floor-to-ceiling plate-glass window was of the blue infinity pool and the sea beyond. He left her to go to the bathroom. She found her cellphone and refitted the battery. Seconds later it signaled an SMS message.

"Go girl! You're doing great. Stay with it. We'll catch up soon for lunch in the country. xxx"

She stared at the screen. WTF? She double-checked the number but it sure wasn't familiar. It wasn't Camille, Shannon, or her mum. It didn't make any sense. Lunch? Shannon had given her lunch at Bloxington Manor. Her heart leapt. DCI Knightsmith was sending her a message outside of the system, probably on a throwaway phone. She must know that the witness protection operation had been compromised and didn't trust her own team. Did this make things better or worse? Looked like she was off to Milan at least with the blessings of the boss. What more could a girl want?

Chapter 17

"The way you're looking at that pool you want to swim," he said handing her a cup of tea as she sat up in bed.

She looked up at his naked form, his strength, his obviously trained abs and pecs.

"I told you I'm not a marine. It's autumn."

"The pool is heated and there's hot air blowers to warm the air."

"The Metropolitan Police didn't issue me with a swim suit."

"Me neither, we'll have to make do with what we've got. There's no one else here."

She reached out for his thigh as he stood alongside her, running her hand up to tease into his dark pubic hair. His cock pulsed a response, visibly swelling. She took it and slowly closed her hand around his shaft, beginning a motion of accelerating desire.

"Careful girl, you turn me on just looking at you. Don't tease him if you don't mean it."

She wanted to, wanted to watch him shoot his juice, helpless to resist her touch. She stopped and smiled.

"Perhaps I'll save you up for later. I've never swum naked."

"You stopped just in time my little Ishtar, but don't think I'll let you off scot-free."

"A good girl always pays her debts."

They stepped out through the electric sliding glass panels. The air was morning chilled but powerful heaters blasted warmth all around them. She slipped into the pool. The water was heavenly, probably at 85 degrees. How she loved the feeling of freedom on her sex and breasts. She never wanted to swim again wrapped up against such delight. It was good to exercise her body, let the fluidity of the water take away the tension of her muscles. She swam lengths while Randolph practiced his dives from a springboard. He was a god, a seal, a bird. A superman who had filled her, at least said that he loved her. Maybe she could spend the rest of her life in this pool with him. He caught her watching and swept across to her in smooth effortless strokes. He took her breasts and brought them to his chest. He lifted her and carried her to the edge, sitting her with her legs open toward him. His tongue went to her groove. The thrill jolted her back, resting on her arms looking at the blue sky and the sea beyond. She was building towards her peak. He stopped. She looked down to see him smiling up at her.

"Fuck, don't stop," she gasped.

"I might save you up for later, or I might show you mercy."

"Please."

He kissed warmly and deeply into her folds, teasing her lips. The ripples built to tremors as she came, gazing out at the white-topped waves of the ocean. A seabird cried, the sun itself began to warm her skin. His finger had slipped inside her as his tongue soothed and hardened her bursting clitoris. He had her sweet spot and she was helpless, jerking out the pulses of her orgasm onto his kissing lips. God, she was out of control. He slowed and looked up at her. In his eyes she could see his joy at his control and her abandon. He knew how to lead her on, lead her on to that edge and she had no power to stop him. Again she crashed in a mindless cloud of ecstasy, spilling her own juice, squeezing the compulsive contractions of her soul into the warmth and tenderness of his touch.

Her legs hung limply into the water. She needed his hot cock to fill her even though her tension had faded. He smiled and swam to the far side of the pool as she slipped in. He had pulled himself out and was standing, his cock huge but subsiding.

"Unfinished business darling," he said.

"Randolph, that was sheer selfish lust. I've never ever come like that."

He drew her to him and kissed her lips.

"And we've only just begun. Hold on for when I really get to know your needs and fantasies."

She let herself melt into his arms. She was in his control and she could *not* hold back. Perhaps the luxury of these surroundings, the power and ease of living with infinite wealth had also seduced her. She looked into his eyes and knew differently. She wanted him if for no more than the joy he could give her body. Billionaire or broke; she wanted him.

"We have a car in about thirty minutes. You started something earlier that'll keep me perky all day," he said with a sexy smile. "For now, let's get out of here."

Fuck! Police were at the door. Through the glass she could see two young uniformed muscular Portuguese police officers. She noted their Polizia badges and big caliber sidearms hanging from belt holsters. Beyond them was what looked like a regular Volkswagen police car with roof-mounted blue lights.

"Shit. Randolph, there's armed cops out there."

"They're two minutes early. Let's go."

"What? We're heading for Faro airport."

"Yup, that's right. Sackman-Platinum do a lot of business in Portugal. The president likes to make sure we're safe, that's all. There's bandits out there, baby."

She picked up her own case and opened the door. She could never have imagined his world. She slid into the back seat. Randolph joined her and took her hand. God, he was a dish. Tanned, tall, relaxed and dressed in a charcoal Ted Baker jacket and dark Versace pants. Knowing it was there, she could trace the shape of his Walther PPK in his shoulder holster. What kind of banker had the balls to carry a firearm in a police car? How the hell were they going to clear airport security? The cops chatted in jerky English but seemed very relaxed even as they hit the main roads at high speed, lights and sirens at full blast. They hurtled past the normal airport traffic holdups and halted at a gate leading straight onto the runway. A Platinum-Sackman full size Boeing 747-8 airliner was waiting with engines running. Crew in platinum-colored uniforms came to carry their baggage. This wasn't like standing in line at airport security at London Heathrow. She wanted to tell herself she didn't like this, felt unworthy of such special treatment. But she *did* like it. She was beginning to love it.

"This plane is huge. It's like a jumbo," she said.

"Yeah. Trump bought a new plane but it's a single-decker. I expect to stay in front of every race. We upgraded to a double just in case I ever found a girl gorgeous enough to take upstairs," he said.

She was definitely beginning to love it. He was hot for her and bursting to come. This could be a good time to play bad cop.

They strapped in to forward facing armchairs as the plane lifted off. Two lovely girls with sleek long platinum hair served coffee.

"It's about a three-hour hop to Milan so let me show you around."

The body of the plane was set out like a luxurious office with desks and terminals.

"If the USA were hit with a nuke we could still trade world markets from here," he explained.

"You'd have to focus on what matters I guess. Wouldn't a nuke attack disturb the markets?"

"Sure, but disruption leads to huge value changes and that means the sharp guy can scoop big. If I expected a nuke I'd be buying canned food, fresh water, and weapons to protect my investment. Big trouble is big cash if you're the right side of the deal."

"And big losses if you're not."

"If you're the wrong side of the deal you shouldn't be in the business. Simple."

"Sometimes I really, really loathe you. I feel squalid for wanting you."

"Squalor is good for business too. Where there's squalor there's desperate poor guys looking for a chance, any way up, any way out. That's the type of personnel we can use. If all else fails we've got businesses to sell them self-help books."

"Are you really so callous or are you just playing the heartless big shot because you're aboard your flying penis symbol?"

"All life's an acting job, Kaitlyn. You're a sweet loving girl, but you stick on that police uniform and show a karate fist to the world. See it this way. I'm leveling with you about what this sort of business is about. Sackman-Platinum don't do cheesy PR of Hollywood types giving rice to hungry kids or sports stars cuddling rescued puppies. We do wealth, *wealth*. If you want it beyond all else, we're the top. We climb the highest heights, we suck the rancid sewers. That's how we attract some of these very challenging clients."

"You sit on a golden plate like a piece of stinking shit with a logo and the flies just home in."

"I love that picture. Sure, they lay their eggs, see their maggots grow and we keep a few. We use them as bait to catch big fish, big honest clean cash ocean fish and that's what we eat ourselves. We eat rich and we shit rich. The flies just keep on eating shit 'cause that's the only taste they like."

"Have you ever thought of being a professor of economics?"

"Hey, honey, that'd be great wouldn't it? You and me in a little cottage somewhere like Oxford, Cambridge, Harvard, Yale. Me coming home on my bicycle from giving a lecture to egghead kids and nibbling crumpets and marmalade."

"To be honest it sounds like heaven."

"You're right but it would depend on the marmalade. I only like thick cut chunky."

"I never know how to take you," she said, annoyed with the way he'd changed tone. He took her in his arms.

"Kaitlyn, the things I say are the truth about this business, not necessarily the truth about me. You'll have to judge me on what I do and you've got instincts and experience enough to do that. I trust and respect you for that. I'm telling you that this is a ruthless business. It's not cruel to the world, it's indifferent. Nobody cries on a shrugging shoulder. You've no idea how I long for things to be different. But they aren't."

"Like I'm judging you as a man who tossed a hand grenade in a car and killed four men."

"Or rubbed out four arms-dealing child-rapist vermin millionaires who'd kidnapped a handicapped woman and were there to torture and kill me. The show you see at the ball game or theater depends on where you sit."

"Are you claiming to be some kind of vigilante?"

"I'm too expensive to hire as a vigilante. I'm just a humble guy with a great gorgeous reason to stay alive forever. Let's take a look upstairs."

She sighed inwardly. Everything about him yelled NO. Everything about him yelled YES. This was not a straightforward man. With her he was unselfish, loved to give, loved to bring her pleasure, maybe more than seeking his own. Sure, that could be a power play to make her beg to fill the craving he created in her. His brain was razor sharp and unsentimental. For Christ's sake he was one of the richest men in the world and all done on his intelligence and toughness. Some of the things he said seemed like hints he wanted her to pick up. She knew that, maybe just believed that because he was so bloody gorgeous. Could beauty and truth in themselves be a scam? She took his hand and smiled.

"Now, where did I get to with you this morning?"

They climbed the spiral stair to the upper deck. Nothing could ever have prepared her for the opulence of the scene in front of her eyes. Thick carpet, tapestries, a huge four-poster bed, chandeliers, old master oil paintings, an original Picasso. She walked through into the ensuite bath and shower room. Every fitting was in gold, every surface was exquisite gray marble. A huge sunken bath appeared to be tiled in gold. The bidet was a bowl of gold. She had to smile. They were flying at 38,000 feet, over seven miles. She glanced out of the window to see mountains far below.

She sat down on the edge of the bed and beckoned him over. He stood in front of her as she unzipped his fly. His cock was already erect and straining for release. She eased in, stroking his balls. He sighed and rested a hand on her head. It seemed far naughtier to touch him while he was clothed. She undid the belt and set him free closing her hand around his shaft. The tip was wet with his juice. She sensed the musk of male as she ran her tongue along his length until his gasp urged her to draw him in, licking up the divide of his glans. He trembled as she quickened her motion, sliding her hand up and down his hard flesh. Pings of lust were pulsing in her own sex. Her panties were dampening as she drew more juice from his tip, as his sounds became more urgent. Suddenly he pulled away, pressing her back onto the platinum silk sheets of the bed. He pulled off her leggings and drew her panties aside. His hand brushed her soaking love button as he drove in his cock to fill her belly with his heat. She started to release, the blur of musk and passion ripping away her restraint. His lips came to taste his own wetness on hers. He bucked and arched his back as he gripped her pelvis hard against him. He shuddered his release deep and deeper into her, the thrill pushing her over the edge into a shriek of orgasm. Still his rigid pushing cock pulsed out his seed as her aftershocks shivered the length of her body. To come with this man was almost too powerful. In his presence she was always aroused, ready to surrender to her own desires. Desires that somehow subliminally he planted in her mind. She hadn't expected him to keep control of himself. Yet he wanted her, to make love to her more than just to release. Many men would have seen her as no more than a hand, a mouth bringing him pleasure. Randolph was a sharer, a lover. Could a man who wanted to share and love with her be an entirely different man toward the rest of the world? She knew the answer she wanted. But she didn't know the answer.

For a few delicious minutes they lay together like innocent babes wrapped in warmth and sleep.

"You're my woman and you just can't help it. I love you," he said in his deep slow voice.

God, how lovely it was to feel the security of his fearless hard body spooned into hers. How wonderful to hear him talk of love. How she wanted to give that knee jerk "love you too" response.

"I love the man I see. I love the man who makes me feel this way. When I know the true heart of that man I'll know if I love him."

He laid her flat and rolled above her. His eyes were kind and serious.

"Then I've no fear of disappointment if I've judged you right," he said.

"You don't have too many doubts about yourself do you?"

"No."

"One day you're going to get something badly wrong and I really don't want that."

"What could happen to me with you to look after me?"

"If you're putting your trust in me, heaven help you, Randolph Quinn. Unlike you, I'm human, fallible. I actually have self-doubt and uncertainty."

"But that's fantastic. You've got everything you say I'm missing. First day I met you in that police car I told you we could be a team."

"You're a slippery lizard."

"Let me lick you," he said, running his tongue up her neck.

How could she not laugh with him?

"I'm going to hit that seven-mile-high golden bidet," she said.

They had re-dressed and gone back downstairs as a voice spoke on the intercom in a smooth American accent.

"This is your captain, Reg Hitchcock, beginning descent into Milano Malpensa airport. It's about fifty-eight degrees with clear skies. We should be on the ground in about fifteen minutes."

He took her hand and spoke to her in a firm voice.

"I'm hoping this little trip will be worth it. My plan is to put an end to all this violence and trouble. I want you at my side, but you're free to go. You've seen the sort of situation that can happen and nothing is certain in this world. I love you enough to say goodbye."

"You're going into danger aren't you?"

"I can't always assess all the angles, that's all."

"I didn't do geometry at school."

"Me neither."

She studied his handsome face, felt the instinct in her gut churn with the passion of him. Her boss at Scotland Yard was privately on her side and wanted her to stay with it.

"We'd better work as a team then," she said.

Chapter 18

The big jet taxied to the edge of the airport. At the foot of the steps waited a silver Alfa Romeo Giulia. A glance at the window glass told her the vehicle was armored. Ahead of her, Randolph slowed and looked around, his body alert and tense. The smartly dressed driver stepped out.

"*Bongiorno* Signor Quinn," he said.

"Where's Fabio?"

"This morning he was sick. I often stand in for him."

The olive-skinned guy smiled, caught her eye as he ran his hands down the gorgeous mid-blue jacket of his fashion suit. Randolph smiled back and eased his hand into the small of her back to direct her into the rear seat of the car.

"You know where we're going?"

"Si, *certo*."

The car moved away, speeding across the tarmac and through a raised barrier manned by a soldier. Soon they were out in the bustle of traffic. Randolph flicked her a glance and then at the door. He gave her hand a squeeze. She'd already picked up on his body language. He was coiled like a cobra ready to spring.

"Hey, I've left my briefcase on the plane. Can I be a real pain in the ass and go back for it?"

Kaitlyn watched the suspicious eyes of the driver in the rear view mirror.

"I'm not sure, *signor*."

Randolph gave her a nod as his hand went inside his jacket. She caught sight of the Walther PPK.

"How not sure? I'm the boss. Just do it."

The driver floored the gas pedal, seeming to panic. They were about to hit the freeway. In a flash Randolph pulled his gun and stabbed it into the back of his neck.

"Don't for a minute think I won't use this. *Capisce?*"

Kaitlyn was aware of a Fiat van drawing alongside.

"Fuck this, Randolph, they've got a bloody machine gun."

"Stop the fucking car," yelled Randolph.

The driver stamped on the brakes. Kaitlyn went for the door release but the driver quickly activated the child locks. The Fiat van was pulling across in front of them, doors opening. No chance of escape on foot. In an instant the Walther PPK spat fire into the driver's neck. He slumped forward into the steering wheel as Randolph hauled him sideways toward the front passenger seat. He had the strength and aggression of a bull.

"Climb across him and drive."

Her heart pumped with wild mouth-drying adrenalin. The engine was running but the driver's legs were blocking the pedals. She forced herself into the gap as bullets began to slam into the body and windshield. She clambered over the seat and forced her leg down toward the gas pedal. The steering wheel was jammed down onto her thighs. She reached for the gear shift and ripped it into drive. She pushed down onto the dead guy's foot. The car spun away, swerving around the Fiat van and the guys firing from automatic weapons. She caught the sign Autostrada dei Laghi. She guessed that meant a freeway with no easy exit. She tried to find the brake but the floor area was blocked with legs and feet. The speed was building and building.

"I'm going to take the shoulder, pull it out of drive and put the fender along the barrier to kill the speed okay."

"You're the boss. Don't forget to use your signals and mirrors."

This guy wasn't for real. What sort of man was this? Fearless, ruthless, loving, comedian, murderer?

She checked behind her. Shit; the Fiat van was behind in the distance. She looked for any sort of escape route. If she stopped they were trapped in the car. The armor would keep them out for a few minutes at best. She was at 110 miles per hour on the shoulder and had no brakes, all the while sitting on a still warm dead body for Christ's sake. Ahead was an exit ramp. Her eyes shot to the overheads, Como, Chiasso, Lentate. The foreign names doubled her feelings of alienation from everything that was happening to her. This was not her life, but for now it was the only life to lead. A van load of murderous thugs was only a minute behind just to keep her focused. As she squealed the tires on the curve of the ramp she jammed the shift lever to neutral and eased the left side fender into the safety barrier.

"Randolph, can you get the handbrake?"

He reached over the top of the body and pulled it up with some kind of superhuman strength. The vehicle slowed. She steered harder into the barrier. They were approaching a junction with a route carrying fast heavy traffic. Not too many choices now. She forced the wheel hard left and thumped the car hard against the metal. At last the rear end spun out and they came to a halt across the road.

"Get out and run," he said.

She didn't need that instruction. She was jammed on top of the dead driver. Randolph ripped open her door and dragged her out, the length of her shins bruising against the steering wheel. She didn't even think of yelling. They scrambled down a grass bank into a wide dry ditch. Ahead was a wire mesh fence. Randolph sprinted in front and crashed into one of the metal stakes bending it to an angle.

"Keep running, you'll make it," he yelled.

She hurtled forward, their joint weight flattening the mesh. In front of them now was a big industrial building. She was reading the word TIGRO on the roof just as a bullet whined over their heads. A glance behind told her three big guys were out of the Fiat van and charging toward them. A cacophony of car horns had started on the blocked exit ramp as the Italian drivers began to vent their frustration. For sure it wouldn't be too long before the cops showed up. Just maybe the thugs would think that through as well. She caught the sound of distant sirens, probably not connected but if they were going to get lucky, it had to be now.

"Lie flat, Randolph."

She dove onto her stomach as they reached a patch of long wild grass, and turned to look back. Sure enough their pursuers had retreated to their van. Sirens grew louder as an ambulance sped up the main track of the freeway and away into the distance. Fortune had intervened this once at least.

"I guess this would be a good time to have an Uber taxi app," he said.

She looked at him as he lay alongside her, breathless, bloody lipped from his impact with the fence.

"Just what is this Randolph? Don't you care? Don't you see the death, the violence and the hopelessness of it all? You killed that guy in cold blood."

"He was kidnapping us. My guess is that the proper driver is dead."

"We need to talk. I can't go on."

"Promise, we'll talk tonight over a pasta like you couldn't even dream and a Chianti plump with summer sun."

He was smiling as he looked into her eyes. Could it be that he'd turned her into a violent criminal on the run and she hadn't even noticed?

"One problem, my sweet lover and murderer, is that I have no clothes, no possessions, no nothing whatsoever."

"Why are women always so hung up on details. This is Milano. We'll find you some old rags to wear."

Her ears caught the sound of a helicopter, almost certainly police. The long grass gave them no cover from above.

"I don't imagine we're thinking of handing ourselves into the polizia or whatever they are here?"

He put on a thoughtful face.

"Mafia? Cousins in the cops? Uncle Scarface married to the judge's niece? Your decision my lovely."

"Let's get out of here."

"I knew you'd see it my way."

"I can't believe I'm here with you. I need to walk away from this now."

He was smiling. He was gorgeous. She wanted him so much that she ached in her bones to possess him. He was the only man who could give her the buzz and joy of sexual love. He was strong, courageous, and intelligent. If only he weren't a murdering criminal.

She turned her attention toward the building ahead. Big trucks with semi-trailers sat with their doors against loading bays.

"Can you call anyone to pick us up?"

"Yes, but if those guys killed Fabio the proper driver, who knows what they know about us? We can assume they know where we were headed so we sure aren't headed there now."

"What do you mean by us?"

"Sackman-Platinum or me or the heroic beautiful blond who just keeps showing up."

"You're full of shit, Randolph."

"Lucky not too full; that was scary back there."

She found herself laughing. The humor was crude but from her own place in life, the same place as his. A south London boy and a south London girl grown up from the same down at heel home. With this man she was at home with or without his wealth and looks. She could understand and respect him, even if they lived out the rest of their lives in different prisons. And that would be if by some small chance they survived at all.

"Pin your ears back, mister. One of those trucks in front of us is running the motor. Looks like the driver is getting a coffee. We're going to walk across that yard like we're management consultants, discussing the transport business. You with me so far?"

"You're so sexy when you go strict and managerial."

"We'll slide over to the truck and clamber up. Not fast not dramatic. I'll take the wheel and we're out of here with a battering ram that nobody's going to stop."

"You can't drive a thing like that. These babies are forty-four tons and bend in the middle"

"Why not? I'm a gorgeous dumb blond with a truck license. I was driving my uncle's fairground trucks when I was ten. Met police traffic officers get trained for anything. Let's go."

She watched his face. She needed him to believe her. Deep down she knew this was a long shot but yet it thrilled her. This was like the very best police work but with no paperwork.

"I respect you, Kaitlyn. I trust you. I'll follow your lead. And, you know, thanks."

His reply had been serious and slow. Here she was, a cop already implicated in a string of crimes. She was about to steal a truck to escape from a murder scene. Well, when you're soaked what the fuck is a bit of rain?

They walked across the wide open space, pointing at the trucks and the depot as if in discussion. A tractor unit pulled away, Randolph gave a small wave in greeting to the driver. The guy waved back. Through the open doors she could see forklift trucks skidding around and workers loading pallets. She saw the white Renault tractor unit. It was older than most of the others but the motor was running. The cab was empty. The loading bay door behind the semi-trailer was closed. She nodded at him and walked to the driver's door. She climbed up and settled into the seat as Randolph clambered up from the other side. She checked out the controls. It was an old-fashioned stick shift gearbox. The cab was a mess, reeking of diesel fuel and cigarette smoke. Now she understood. It was the shunter truck probably with a faulty battery so they didn't shut it down.

"Reach out the window and pull that mirror in a little," she said, adjusting her own side. She could see him nodding.

"You're a pro. Will you marry me?"

"Fuck off, Randolph."

"Please."

She sighed and engaged second gear. If the semi was empty she'd soon know. She felt the bite of the clutch and the front of the truck lift away. She shifted smoothly to fourth, watching the trailer follow her in the mirror.

"Don't forget your seat belt, officer."

"Fuck off, Randolph."

"You keep saying that."

She approached an exit gate with a closed barrier. A guy inside a cabin was reading a newspaper. Idly he pushed a button and the red and white pole rose to set them free. She swung left and concentrated hard as she cleared a line of parked trucks.

"You impress me, Mrs Quinn."

"Fuck off, Randolph."

"How many lucky girls on this planet get a proposal of marriage from a billionaire while they're at the wheel of a forty-ton truck?"

"How many murderous criminal billionaires get told to fuck off?"

"You're right. Our situation is completely unique. Something like me has never happened to you and something like you has never happened to me. Normally I'd never have sex with a truck driver."

She gave another sigh of exasperation.

"Okay, big shot. Where the fuck are we going? It won't be long before every cop in Milan is looking for this heap of smoking shit."

"In *bocco al lupo*. Take the freeway E62 straight in to downtown Milan."

"You speak Italian?"

"*Si*, I watched all the Godfather films."

"And then what?"

"Okay, top level conference. Something went wrong this morning. I was coming to Milan to meet a guy who can resolve all this petty local politics. Some bad guy knew I was coming and hijacked my driver. Now I'm outside of my own trusted loop because I don't know what the penetration is. You're already outside your trusted law and order loop. We're united in a mutual loneliness that can only be ended by pasta, smooth red wine and a night of abandoned *amore*. Do you have a credit card?"

"Don't tell me I've got to pay."

"You don't have to, but billionaires don't carry small change. We hire people to handle that kind of stuff."

"You really are an arrogant prick."

"True, but my own credit cards carry my name and there are those who are looking for that name. If we use your cheap trash Mastercard no one will need to know who you're with. If you're good and agree to marry me I'll get Sackman-Platinum to meet your expenses."

"Fuck off, Randolph."

"There you go again, and there was me thinking you were original."

She took the ramp out onto the freeway, easing the truck up into its high ratio end of the gearbox. The air servo hissed its mechanical music that once she had known so well. She glanced at his handsome face. She was doing it. She was doing this for her lover. Doing something he could not do for all his wealth. Doing something no woman whom he could ever meet could or would do for him. He reached across the cab and touched her forearm as she held the wheel.

"I admire you. I trust you. I love you," he said in a slow deep voice.

She checked her mirrors and made a gear shift. She flicked him a glance.

"I'd love you to shut the fuck up. Don't distract the driver okay."

Chapter 19

The roads and streets of Milan were getting narrower, busier, and slower. She'd never been to Italy, but she loved it already. The tall grand and sombre buildings looked down on human anarchy with a warm tearful smile. The world is mad and shifting, so sanity is to dance in perfect time to its certainties; desire, passion, heartbreak, and love.

"It's about time to ditch the truck. I'm guessing you know this place," she said.

"Sure, we're in Foro Buonaparte. You'll see Parco Sempione coming up on the right. There should be some quiet spot."

She steered the huge machine through the traffic, struggling to avoid tram cars that didn't seem to stop for anything. She was rolling along a route with names like Viale Emilio Elmagna, Viale Moliere. How strange these foreign sounds were as she tried to pronounce them as a way of distracting herself from her stress. She saw an entrance into the park with high iron gates swung open. The road itself was narrow with cars parked on either side. With luck she could fit the cab through but the closer she got, the less sure she was. She put on a bit of speed. If she was wrong then a bit of momentum would push her through. Maybe.

"You're an absolute star with this thing," he said.

"You'd better hope so."

She lined up on the center of the gap and waited for an impact. Halfway through she checked her mirrors. She guessed she had a couple of inches to spare. Branches of trees rattled and scraped on the roof as she stopped, operated the parking brake with a hiss of air, and turned to Randolph.

"Some poor bastard's going to have a horrible job to back out of here."

"I can't believe the way you handled it."

"I don't know where the fuck we are or where we're going."

"It's a lovely day for two young lovers to stroll through the park. I love these stolen moments when no one knows where we are."

She shook her head and jumped down. People must have noticed the arrival of a monster truck but no park attendants were shouting or waving. He scampered around to join her, took her hand, kissed her lips and set off along a path.

"*Ti amo, bella*," he said.

"Just like that. Another smooth day at the office. Randolph, you just killed another man. That's five since I met you."

"Hmm, that's the trouble when you've got a beautiful girl to impress. Work, work, work just to keep her happy."

"Don't you care?"

He stopped for a moment and looked her in the eyes.

"I'd give anything for this world to be a better place but it isn't and nothing's about to change in the future."

"So how many bodies do we need to pile up to bring about your notion of paradise?"

"Once people stop trying to kidnap, torture, and kill me it'll be over. I'm an honest business man, a banker."

"With an automatic James Bond-style gun in a shoulder holster."

"Yeah well, James is an OK guy but he always tries to copy me."

"So how can your life go on from here? You and I are going to have to account for the killings, the damage, the theft of motor vehicles, etcetera, etcetera."

"What does your DCI Shannon Knightsmith want you to do?"

"She wants me to stay with you but I think that's her personal position, not the official line."

"Because we can't trust the cops and she can't trust the cops. Crooks have so much data on so many people that anyone can be corrupted or simply blackmailed. I mean good people who aren't greedy but maybe a straight judge, priest, or cop looks at a gay porn clip, or bought an embarrassing sex toy, uses a dating site, or lied on a CV. The Internet has brought everyone many things, but believe me, it's a bonanza to every crook and extortionist on the planet."

"So, you've got the golden key to infinite wealth and these business associates of yours believe that you have stolen it from them. Maybe you have stolen it?"

"My wealth, Sackman-Platinum's wealth, comes from our wise investments of money deposited with us. Many world class banks would not deal with these gentlemen."

"That's because they're criminals, terrorists, and murderers, and probably rape their grannies."

"Hey, you should be working for us. You've hit the target client profile right in the bull's eye."

"So none of this can ever end. We could never have any sort of life together."

"Wow, it's great you're thinking of a life together. Are you trying to put ideas in my head? You're a bit forward, young woman, considering we've only just met."

She smiled faintly, realizing she'd given away something from her heart that she was not about to admit to him.

"I don't want to die, and I don't want you to die."

He pulled her into his arms, fixed his eyes on hers and kissed her lips. She let herself melt into him, feeling his love, yes that must be what she felt in him. She felt absorbed by him, fixed, and secure in the strength of his arms.

"You're an evil bastard, Quinn."

"For showing you your true desire and feeling?"

"For being an evil arrogant bastard."

"You were brilliant today. I don't know any operator who could have pulled off an escape like that."

"We got lucky."

He continued to hold her. He'd called her an *operator* once before. What did he mean? She kept the question inside her head. First she had to think what to do. In the pocket of her jeans she had her cellphone, driving licence, her Mastercard and a one-pound British coin. She was more or less at her credit limit. Christmas was coming but the chances of being alive long enough to worry about buying presents were zero. It was a small comforting thought.

"Why did you come to Milan?"

"To meet with a guy who can end this war. Our friends today don't want peace. They hijacked my car and put their own guy at the wheel."

"How did you know?"

"When my normal driver didn't show I was suspicious, but I played along. The other hoods were nearby, but remember they want me alive. I played along but tested him out when I asked him to go back to the plane. Then I knew we were in trouble."

"There was no plan B was there? We either got lucky or we got the kidnap, rape, torture, and death prize."

"With you beside me how could I have lost? Anyway who needs plan B when you've got a plan C?"

"What's plan C?"

"I told you already. Pasta, Chianti and the thrill of love."

"Anyone in mind for this irresistible date?"

"You just said yes. Now when I was a kid I loved trains and stuff like that. Milano has got trams, so let's take a ride."

"You're not normal."

"But you're in love with me."

She stopped walking, looking up into his calm handsome face. Of course she was in love with him. He was fearless, strong, intelligent, so good-looking that she just wanted to gaze at him. Sure she could be in love with that. They'd come through a lot and how she wanted him, his touch, the urgent thrill of her own body under his gentle control.

"Yes, I'm in love with you. We're going to die probably so I'll admit that and what's to lose? I want you to know that so it's not just a word game of jokey answers. Yes, it's so sad I've fallen for you and we'll never have any sort of chance to explore a proper life. And that just breaks my fucking heart if you really want to know, you arrogant asshole."

Tears flooded out of her. She couldn't stop. Didn't want to stop because just maybe these tears would get through to some man inside the smile and the cocky evasions.

He let out a deep sigh and pulled her to his chest. He didn't try to kiss her but held her tight and warm against him.

"I know. My sweet woman, I know. I have to put on a front. My life is a front. I hate myself not for the way I treat you but for the way I cannot treat you. One day you'll understand that, I promise you. I promise you my absolute trust in you and ask you to trust me. Can you be my goddess Ishtar?"

She'd forgotten the tattoo and the power she'd dreamed it would give her.

"Randolph, just don't let me down. All powerful goddesses can be fucking spiteful."

"Never, and that's a promise. But you have to know you're not my first love."

"Okay tell me her name."

"It wasn't a stupid girl. Trains and trams. Come on, there's a stop over there."

"Where do we get a ticket?"

"We don't. We're crooks."

She held his hand as they ran toward an old-fashioned orange tram that was pulling up at a stop. The sign on the front read "*Duomo.*"

They pushed their way into the crush of passengers, finding a place to grip the smooth metal pole. The car lurched and squealed around bends and points, stopping outside La Scala opera house. The air smelled of perfume and garlic. Immaculate men wore perfect suits with brown suede pointy shoes. Several caught her eye, smiled, or winked. A girl could make her man jealous very easily in Milano. Randolph was grinning at the little pantomime of flirtation she was creating. He leaned in and whispered.

"They trim their nasal hair for an hour every morning and spend two hours a day on the phone to mamma."

"I'm pleased about the nasal hair but no mamma's keeping her little boy from me."

"You got it. I'll send some boys round to wipe out my mum."

"You're not normal."

"Neither's my mum. She'd eat them alive."

"For once I believe you."

"That's because you love me."

"Fuck off."

"You keep saying that."

"You're not normal."

"You keep saying that."

The tram lurched to a stop.

"*Il Duomo. Andiamo,*" he said.

"Do you speak Italian or not?"

"*Si*, like a native, like the pope."

"He's from Argentina."

"Good point, officer, but he's a native in South America just as I am a native in South London."

"Watch my lips. *Do you speak Italian?*"

"*Si. Naturalemente parlo Italiano, ma non sono esperto.* Who wants to be around some bloody show-off?"

His accent sounded perfect. He seemed so at ease here. In her original briefing they'd covered the Camorra Mafia who control much of the Milan fashion business. Randolph was their banker but yet he didn't want to big himself up. He wasn't normal. He joked about danger, but minimized his real self.

"Will you just take a look at that," he said, pointing to the magnificent front of Milan cathedral.

She looked over at the almost mirage quality of the white stone in the bright autumn afternoon sunshine. He took her hand and walked across the piazza. To the left was a magnificent arch leading into a fabulous shopping arcade. The curved roof was made of glass. This place had a self-confidence and a flourish of humanity like a feather in the hat of a poor peasant on a feast day. Tourists swarmed, yet history and wealth stood firm and beckoned to those who had the balls to claim it. She was with a man bold enough and reckless enough to tread the streets of gold or bleed out his life into the cracks between the stones. She loved him. She loved him. In this place, with her hand in his, she loved him.

"I love you," she said.

"Simply? Just like that?"

"What other way?"

For once he looked down. Randolph never looked down. Never. When he looked up his eyes were warm and almost heavy with a tear.

"I didn't deserve that from you. You're better than me, braver than me. I'll love you forever, my sweet woman."

"I've lost the plot, haven't I?"

"The big and the bold don't follow plots they write their own plots. Come on, just point to the fashion name you want and Sackman-Platinum will dress you in the manner worthy of a woman in love."

His arm was around her shoulder, her arm was around his waist as they strolled into the center of the Galleria Vittorio Emanuele. Even the marble floor was magnificent. In a circle around them were the names of the famous brands of the world's fashion catwalks, proclaimed in gold against black marble. Versace, Louis Vuitton, Prada, Gucci, Giorgio Armani.

"Just tell me the name you want and it's yours."

"Christ Randolph, I'm an H&M girl. How should I know?"

"Well, I don't know."

"Prada, the devil wears Prada. Was that a film?"

"God knows? Prada it is. Let's find our hotel. I need to kiss the joy out of your pussy."

"You don't want me to try stuff on?"

"When a man loves a woman there's nothing he can't work out about her."

"Balls."

"Exactly! When a man loves a woman he's worked out she hasn't got balls."

"Okay wise guy, where's the hotel and how are we going to pay?"

"Your little Mastercard will do just fine. As far as I know, no one with a machine gun knows your name."

"I've not got too much credit."

"I'll fix that if we have to."

"Why are we going to a hotel?"

"Because we're anonymous tourists. Something went badly wrong this morning. Until I've checked out my own systems I'm staying right outside it."

They strolled back across the cathedral piazza and along a bustling street. The October sun was still warm, trams clanked, rattled, and squealed among an ad hoc symphony of car horns, church bells and the tap of fashion heels worn by impossibly immaculate women. Sunlight glinted from street cobblestones, wafts of coffee made sensual islands in the sea of movement. They had arrived at a junction. She saw a name she recognized from school days—Via Medici. On the corner was the Hotel Ariston.

"Looks like the sort of place, remember that name," he said.

Behind the hotel was another hotel, the Carrobbio. She watched Randolph's eyes switching between the two buildings. He took her hand and walked back to the Ariston. He spoke in fast Italian to the beautiful girl on the desk.

Several times she caught him giving his name. She smiled wrote down some details, having difficulty not staring at his looks and body. Bitch. He finished the conversation.

"OK. *Grazie mille. A presto, ciao.*" He turned, took her hand and walked back into the street. "I've told her all our stuff has been delayed at the airport and it's coming by courier. Now let's check into the Carrobbio. I'll need your card and you'll be doing the talking, *capisce*?"

"To do what?"

"To check in. Tell them your luggage is being delivered by taxi."

"What did you just do in the other hotel?"

"I've laid a little trap, my dear. And I'm going to be in the just the right place to see if it springs."

How the hell could anyone live like this? As soon as she got to a room she was going to get a drink and call the boss.

The guy on the desk spoke perfect English. She handed over her driving licence as ID, Randolph handed over his passport and stayed back, reading tourist leaflets. He made a drinking motion to his mouth.

"Could we have champagne brought to our room?" she asked.

"*Si, certo*," replied the concierge with a broad smile.

Well, that will have exploded her credit. She half expected the card to burst into flames.

His hand rested just above her ass, not quite indecently as he guided her to the lift.

"Champagne, *signora*; you are so generous. I was considering making love to you anyway but I will have to repay you somehow."

"You're a cocky jerk."

She opened the room door and flopped exhausted onto the bed. Did she even want sex? How long before some hoods turned up and smashed their way in?

A minute later a waiter arrived with champagne. Randolph lifted the phone and asked for an outside line. For some reason he was now speaking only in English.

"Hi Giovanni, I'm at the Ariston Hotel on Via Medici. Can you fix me a car in about two hours? That's great thanks." He hung up and placed another call. "Hey Giorgi? It's good to hear you, man. I'm at the Carrobbio Hotel on Via Medici. I've

111

got a gorgeous size 10 girl who wants Prada. Yeah, the whole works. She's dining out tonight with a fabulous guy called Lee Smith, so she wants to look good enough to eat. Get me a jacket and a suit, shirt, underwear, socks. Once you're sorted get a Louis Vuitton suitcase and take a cab round here and I'll buy you a drink. Well, I'll buy you a drink if you can bring me some cash; not too much, a thousand euros or so. Try and get here in an hour and a half from now. Yeah, Giorgi I guess you know there's been some local difficulty so keep yourself alert. I love you man."

He hung up. She shook her head.

"Are you ever going to tell me what the hell you are and what's going on?"

"I'm Randolph Quinn, International Vice President of Sackman-Platinum Bank. We have a slight customer service issue and I'm dealing with the matter."

"You know, I just don't know what to believe. This is like some thriller movie with secret agents and code names. Who's that guy Giorgi?"

"His full name is Giorgi Dzneladze . We call him Giorgi Deez because we can't pronounce that. He works for us. He fought the Russians as a teenage guerrilla when they invaded Georgia in 2008. He showed up working in a pizza joint in Rome. I saw he had talent."

"How old were you then?"

"Twenty, I think. Banking's a tough game so you need to be young."

"So you recruited some guy who fought Russian army tanks in the streets to work as a banker."

"I can always see talent. I chose you, too."

"Randolph, I'm not a recruit for anything. I'm a Metropolitan police traffic cop working as your bodyguard."

"If you're nice to me I could still get you a job at the bank."

"So who was the other guy you called?"

"Giovanni, he's one of our guys in Milan. He's not an inside operator. He's a fixer for stuff like transport and reservations. He assigns the drivers their jobs and cars."

Kaitlyn had a sudden flashback to her real life as a cop. She thought it through. Randolph had set a trap to see if this Giovanni was involved with the bad guys they'd met at the airport. In a bit less than two hours someone was going to turn up at the hotel next door. They would soon know.

"I can see the wheels of your mind whizzing around," he said with a sexy smile. "Let's open the champagne."

While he popped the cork of the Bolinger Special Cuvee, she thought hard, watching his strong hands, the flatness of his honed abdomen, the power of his arms and shoulders. A delicious deep tingle flickered on the edge of her focus. Just the look of him was making her wet. What the fuck could she do with herself?

"I'm going to keep asking you questions until I get some sensible response, Randolph. Tell me straight, what's your next move?"

"I've come to see a man who can resolve these customer service issues."

"Does this mysterious man kill people?"

"You'd have to ask him that. I'm a banker."

"What's his name?"

"Valmir Rudovic. He's Albanian. He runs a little people trafficking, drugs and prostitution operation, mainly in Germany. He owns a lot of farms, castles, and a small airline operating in South America. He's got twenty-nine billion dollars on deposit with Sackman-Platinum. Our friends from London, Paris, and this morning work for him. He wants us to believe that his thugs are the local Italian Camorra Mafia. I've told him he could lose his deposit account overnight if we called the FBI. He thinks we need to talk. I suggested Milan because the local crooks keep a big wedge of cash with us and they're not looking for drama on their territory. If we need some allies, we've got numbers to call."

"Fucking hell, Randolph. Are you telling me that our friendly neighborhood back up team is the Camorra Mafia?"

"Sure. They're pros. If the Camorra wanted me I'd be dead meat by now. These Albanians are a van load of murderous slobs with a second-hand machine gun from the Yugoslavian war."

"But this Valmir Rudovic wanted to meet you for a business chat, but still tried to snatch us at the airport."

"That's because he's a dumb psychopath. Tell me what kind of guy works for five years in his business and has only twenty- nine billion dollars to show for it? He's a loser."

"But you're going to meet him all the same?"

"Yeah, in my own way and in my own time. Tomorrow I might want a lovely girl on my arm and maybe catch some opera at La Scala, maybe buy her the greatest ice cream in the world, maybe stay in bed all day. I'll need to check out the currency exchanges. Every Trump tweet sends a shiver through the markets. The quick little birdie can always grab a crumb or two."

"What sort of crumb?"

"A tweet against North Korea hammers the Japanese yen. For a holding of a couple of billion I could pocket a million if I can sell before the tweet and buy after the tweet."

"How can you know what Trump has in mind?"

"It's easy, he wrote a book to tell the world how he thinks. I've read it."

"You really are a banker aren't you?"

"Did you think I wasn't?"

"Sometimes I've thought you're a murderous crook."

"Now you're splitting hairs."

He poured champagne. She slugged it down, two glasses, three....

"I'm going to get a shower."

"Great minds think alike."

He soaped her back, her front, soothed and smoothed her breasts as he kissed her. He washed her hair, slid his hand to her groove to make her groan and almost double over with the sudden surge of her orgasm. He filled her from behind, teasing her nipples. She ran her hand down her belly to pulse her clit with the rhythm of his thrusts. She was beginning to come but the champagne was working inside her body.

"Randolph, I need to wee."

"You're in the shower so go for it. I do."

She was coming, couldn't stop. She was working her clitoris as he brought his lips and tongue to her neck. Oh God, she was releasing as his cock drove into her, hitting that slightly naughty spot. She was gushing, feeling her own heat on his hard cock.

"That's so sexy. I love your sweet wet pussy. Let it all go. You're making me come. You're making me come."

114

A wave of ecstasy rippled through her body. Her wet heat flowed unashamed as he drove to her depth, pulsing out his cum into her sucking belly.

"Fuck cum, fucking shoot in my pussy," she groaned.

"You're too sexy," he growled.

At last she turned off the water and let him hold her drained body in his tireless sculpted arms.

"I'd like to think I'd feel a bit embarrassed at least."

"What? You're a hot lover woman like no man could ever dream. If ever we're apart I'm going to be jerking off crazy reliving that sweet gush."

"You're a lover, Randolph. I lose grip of everything when you touch me."

"Just remember that tonight. Every pretty boy in Milano would die for your pussy but only one man can love you properly."

"What pretty boys?"

"Like all those guys on the tram, wanting to kneel down and kiss those sweet pink juicy lips of love, beg and implore you for your hot wet woman love."

"Like that gorgeous girl at the hotel next door wanting to drive her tongue down your throat."

"I didn't notice."

"Balls."

"You keep saying that."

"You're a ruthless killer."

"You're a mean karate cop."

"I prefer karaoke."

"You're a pretty mean singer too. You need a record deal and a manager."

"Fuck off."

"You keep saying that."

Chapter 20

She was still drying from the shower when she heard a knock at the door and then Randolph talking in Italian to a strong sounding guy. She pulled on the complimentary bathrobe and stepped out.

"Kaitlyn, I'd like you to meet Giorgi Dzneladze. He's a top man at the bank and a true friend."

She studied a tall guy of about her own age, fair-skinned with short cut hair. He had a broad smile and prominent cheekbones. His eyes were quick and intelligent, his body hard and wiry. He had placed a Louis Vuitton suitcase and a leather Gucci holdall on the floor.

"*Piacere*, my great pleasure to know you, *signora*."

His voice was almost lyrical with a mix of accents. He wore a stylish deep brown leather jacket and impeccable pressed beige Armani pants. Prada sunglasses hung from a white silk shirt. She caught the slight bulge of a shoulder holster. Well, he's a banker so of course a James Bond gun comes with the office chair.

"Let's leave Kaitlyn to try on her wardrobe. There's still some sun so let's sit downstairs with a drink."

Giorgi nodded and smiled. She could see in his face that he was looking for some action. So this guy had been a teenage rebel soldier as the Russian army had bulldozed his country. What did she know of life compared to a man like that? What was it they say? Never judge a man until you've walked a mile in his moccasins. She was pretty sure he would die for Randolph. Selfishly and horribly she knew she would want him to do just that if it came to it. She knew what they wanted to do. They wanted to see who showed up at the hotel next door and they were just going to sit there and sip a beer like it was a couple of business men, maybe even bankers.

"Take your time, gorgeous," said Randolph with a wink as the boys stepped out to play.

She opened the suitcase. This was like the biggest and best dressing up box in the world. There was Prada underwear, a turquoise leather miniskirt, a pair of red velvet Mary Jane shoes, a black top with an emerald crystal pin, a pair of black studded jeans, a pair of patent leather lace-up boots. There was a selection of Kiko Milano makeup in a Bottega Veneta case. There was everything and more.

She sighed to herself. How shallow she had become, loving these gorgeous clothes, forgetting that her lover was sitting downstairs maybe waiting for a shootout with a bunch of killers. He was one of the richest men in the world, for sure the biggest risk taker she'd ever met. Could she allow herself to be pulled along this path of infinite wealth? There was a problem deep in her heart. She loved it, unashamedly loved it. She'd been born to stand in line, wait for the bus in the rain, shop for the bargain deal in Walmart, drag the heavy suitcase up the escalator of life. The plane, the yacht, the chauffeur cars, the respect, the beauty. She loved it. Now she had seen it and touched it she would always long for it. With Randolph in the shower she had just let go, shameless because he wanted it and it had thrilled her just to be so wanton. Wealth was the same stuff. No shame, no fear, no guilt. Could she ever go back now to being a traffic cop, just about getting by? Probably Interpol was looking for her for murder in Paris and now in Milan. She picked up her cellphone and called DCI Shannon Knightsmith. At least she could check in with the boss and pretend she was still a straight cop.

"Kaitlyn, thank god. Are you OK?"

"Sure. Why do you ask?"

"You had a problem at Milan airport."

"It was cool. We killed a guy, crashed the car and so I had to steal a tractor and semi trailer to get away."

"Jesus Christ. Look, I can't really talk right now, I'll call you later."

"Shannon, should I just pull out and come clean about everything? I've done some bad stuff myself."

"You've done what you needed to do at the time. Do as you're fucking well told and just keep doing it, OK. Trust me."

She tossed the phone on the bed. What a crazy conversation. Obviously Shannon wasn't in a position to talk. Then she'd gone all stressed and angry. Could it be that a detective chief inspector of Scotland Yard was giving her permission to kill, steal and lie? In any event, the local cops would follow their own rules. They'd left a dead body in a car on the freeway. There would be fingerprints, CCTV cameras, DNA and if they wanted more, her passport was in the case in the trunk. Suddenly she felt afraid and alone. She needed a friend. She called Camille.

"Where the fuck are you?"

"Milan, but I've been around a bit. Do you remember I asked you to get anything you could on Sackman-Platinum?"

"Sure, it's a bank."

"And?"

"It's a rich bank. The CEO is a woman, Stella Boursellino."

"Yeah, but do they have any criminal connections, money laundering, suspicion of fraud, all that stuff."

"It's a bank and that's it. The US and UK regulators give them a clean bill of health. They're rated A1 on all the charts."

"So what is this Randolph doing?"

"He's a rogue banker who got greedy. He bit off more than he could chew and he's going to get his head blown off, probably sooner rather than later. If you're mixed up with this guy you know my advice."

"So why doesn't the bank just fire him?"

"He's still making them money. It's that simple."

Kaitlyn bit her lip as her mind churned over and over. Maybe Camille was right. Maybe the bank didn't care just so long as the cash came in. She'd talked with Stella Boursellino on board the super yacht and she'd asked her to trust both Randolph and her. DCI Knightsmith had told her to hang in there. In her heart she knew she wasn't a top ace detective. She was a foot soldier who could be duped as well as anyone. For some reason she didn't want to give too much away to Camille.

"Thanks anyway. I'll catch you soon."

"Are you still with him?"

"No, he's off doing some business."

"Where are you staying?"

"Some big mansion. It's somewhere between Milan and Venice I think."

"Just take care, sugar. Get the hell out of there."

"Love you."

She rang off before Camille answered. Something had told her not to give away her location. Now she wasn't even trusting her best friend. She'd thrown her a lie without a second thought. What she needed was a red line. How far would she go to stick with him? She had to set her own feelings aside. There was still right and wrong in the world whatever she felt in her heart and, she had to admit, in her pussy.

She changed into the new sexy Prada underwear and clicked on the Italian news channel Rai24. With her two years of schoolgirl Latin she could decipher that thirty-seven Mafia types of the Rinzivillo clan had been arrested along with some caribinieri police officers and a lawyer. Seemed like a quiet day. She chose the turquoise leather miniskirt, black top and the Mary Jane's. She felt good. Maybe the boys wouldn't want her downstairs. Maybe that would be the best reason for joining them. She grabbed a Gucci Dionysus suede bag from the suitcase. She was wearing at least four months wages but hell, she felt good.

Randolph stood as she appeared on the forecourt of the hotel. He held out his arms in welcome.

"Bloody hell. You're not going out like that. Half of Milan will be gasping."

"Which half?"

"The half with good taste."

She sat down on the outdoor sofa. The boys had Peroni beers in front of them. Both of them were seated to look down the street at the Hotel Ariston. A couple of shrubs in pots gave them cover. Randolph checked his watch and called over to a waiter.

"A Peroni for the lady *per favore*."

"I shouldn't...."

"You're right, but you've got to keep hydrated. It's been a warm day."

He slipped her a wink. He was impossible. He was so, so sexy.

The beer arrived. Giorgi was looking over her shoulder. He stiffened and winked at Randolph.

"We have friends. A Fiat van, three guys. One of them's heading into the hotel."

119

"Now, what a surprise," said Randolph with a smile. "Did you hear the noise as the trap sprung?"

"So what are you going to do?" asked Kaitlyn.

"Watch me," said Giorgi.

He stood up, slid his hand inside his coat and sauntered down the cobbles of Via Medici. He passed the Fiat van and walked casually into the hotel lobby.

"He's harder than steel. He's one of the top pros in the world," said Randolph.

A few seconds later he came out, gun pointed into the back of the guy walking in front of him. They got to the van. Giorgi indicated for the driver to lower his window. He spoke a few words. The driver nodded and nodded. Slowly the man got back into the vehicle while Giorgi trained the gun on the driver. Then he took a cheeky stance a big grin on his face imitating a cop directing traffic. The driver floored the gas and shot up the narrow street past where she was still sitting with Randolph. He took a swig of beer. Giorgi stored his weapon and wandered back.

"I won't stop. See you guys."

He didn't pause but just kept going as if nothing had happened.

"What did he do?" she asked.

"He told them he was from the local Camorra Mafia and that his boys had already grabbed that thieving asshole, Randolph Quinn. He added that they could either have a war or fuck off. Looks like they're natural diplomats after all."

"Now you know that your guy, Giovanni, can't be trusted."

He nodded and tweaked his eyebrow.

"Giorgi never did like him. He'll deal with it."

"I can imagine."

"No, you can't. Even I can't imagine Giorgi in a bad mood."

"I guess it's all part of international finance. I expect this is the sort of stuff you do on an MBA course."

Randolph shook his head and smiled.

"Did we finish that champagne?"

Chapter 21

"I guess you phoned your boss?" said Randolph as they walked hand in hand along Via Medici.

"Of course. I'm just an amateur criminal. The Met police still pay my wages."

"Ah, *capito*. She's pretty cool that Shannon."

"She's gorgeous, beautiful, exotic, smart."

"All things are relative my lovely. All depends on what you're looking at and right now I'm looking at the hottest girl in Milano."

"But you did notice Shannon's beautiful skin, perfect eyes, film-star lips?"

"Can't recall all that. First time I met her she was with her husband."

"What?"

"She's married to Spencer Knightsmith, Earl of Bloxington."

"She told me. You say you met him?"

"Sure, it was at a charity ball at Merchant Taylors Hall in the City of London. It's just a bit exclusive. I was a guest of the governor of the Bank of England. Spencer's an aristocrat so he's a member by right. We've done a few bits of business together. He's a massive guy in commodity trading; you know buy coffee, sell rubber, buy steel, sell copper. He's a completely straight operator. His word is his bond. Don't even think about crossing him though."

"Let me understand this. You do business with Detective Chief Inspector Shannon Knightsmith's husband?"

"Yeah. They invited me down to some great kind of castle for a weekend."

"I know it, I've been there."

"That figures. You have to be real special to be asked."

"So what kind of a deal am I in? Suddenly I get a crumb of information that tells me you're a social pal of my boss. She's a top Scotland Yard detective and you're a crook on the run."

"My lovely, lovely girl. Life is like a hall of mirrors at the fair. What you see depends on where you see it from. Some days I'm the richest man in the world depending on how things trade. I'm not thirty yet. TV producers want me on that Apprentice show. Breakfast shows want me to kiss babies and give them the gift of wealth. I stay right out of sight, because, because my lovely woman ... because I just can't tell you everything even though it's bloody near breaking my heart."

He looked at her in the deep dusk of the late evening. Suddenly his mood was a sombre and still as the buildings of this city.

"Have you already told me too much?"

"Yes, because, because; well to be crude it's like being desperate for a pee. Once you start...."

She laughed.

"You're a cheeky bastard."

"I'm hungry."

"Hypothetically, I love you, Randolph. Let me shout that out and see what echo comes back. Do you love me enough to throw everything aside and square with me about your life, your future, your relationship with my bosses?"

"I'm hungry enough to eat you."

"That's an evasion."

"I know and I'm ashamed of it."

"But it's all I'm going to get?"

"No, you're going to get the best Italian food in Milan. If you want to talk more I'll need a pillow."

"You're a slimy jerk. It's always *mañana*."

"Not in Italy. Tomorrow here is *domani*."

They strolled on along the Via Santa Marta until they stopped at La Fettunta *ristorante*. He led her in to a reserved table. He shook hands with an older man at the desk and did a two-cheek kiss with a waitress. He ordered a Chianti wine and spoke quickly to a waiter in Italian.

"Sackman-Platinum uses this place. For my money it's the best in Milano."

"If they know you, they might give someone a tip that you're here."

"Just accept that these guys are cool. This place is one hundred percent Italian. *Capisce*?"

The food was delicious and nothing like the chain restaurants with Italian names in London. She had a spicy pasta to start and grilled giant prawns to follow. What a life.

What it must be to know places like this, travel like this, speak languages, possess infinite wealth. She had no right to be hungry. She should be crippled by guilt and fear if she thought back on the day let alone back to London, the super yacht and Paris. Yet, she was calm, drawing her own mood from his. Soon enough this would end and there would be a huge price to pay, but here in this moment, nothing but this moment was her life. She felt his warm kind eyes on her face.

"That job you did today was world class. I can't believe you just cruised over to a forty-ton truck, stole it, and drove it into central Milan."

"We didn't have too many options, Randolph. I kind of get creative when I'm being chased by the Albanian Mafia with a machine gun."

He laughed.

"You're world class. Just accept that. Listen, soon, very soon things will be better. Just keep that thought in your mind."

His lips were tight, as if he were struggling with himself to hold something back.

"You want to tell me something don't you? Cops get that feeling when someone wants to confess and get it over with."

"Maybe I just want to tell what you already feel."

"What?"

"That you're the most beautiful woman in the world and I don't deserve you."

She gave him a stare and a tight smile. She'd trodden on his toes, given him a bit of pain and now he was deflecting her. Again.

"You're half right. You don't deserve me."

He reached out both his hands across the table toward her. She couldn't help it. She offered hers into his without hesitation and let her gaze taste him, search down and down into his deep eyes to try and find the truth of him. He had reached out and she had responded with a helpless reflex. She was lost and any resistance was no more than whistling in the dark. She had to find some assertiveness.

"Set aside all that's happened up until now. As of this moment I will not be part of any violence or killing. That is my red line and that is what I mean. If I don't die I'm going to jail but I'm still a good guy, Randolph. I was a cop and now look at me."

"That's what I am doing. The view is fantastic."

"You've got a red line to work to. *Capisce?*"

"I understand. I'll be a good boy."

The look on his face was cheeky, sincerely insincere, daring her to challenge him.

"Red line."

"You keep saying that."

He was simply so handsome that she could not pull her eyes away from him. It wasn't fair. It wasn't fair. Why did the beautiful always get their way, win the deal, get the part, get the girl? She felt a stab of anger toward him merely because of his looks and the undeserved power it gave him. She was beginning to understand the complexity and perversity of her own nature. The champagne and the wine had dulled her focus. There was so much to think about. She needed to draw out a chart to connect up all the clues and events. Randolph was a business associate of her boss's husband. He'd been invited to Bloxington Manor before she'd ever met him. A bell was ringing in her head. DCI Shannon Knightsmith must have known him already, before the car crash and his arrest. Her boss was lying about a lot of stuff. She had pretended not to know about Paris. She had pretended not to know Randolph. Was she corrupt? Was her husband one of Randolph's crooked clients? The idea stuck in her mind. It had to be that. Shannon had ordered her to stay with Randolph not because she wanted him as a witness but because he was a crook who worked with her husband and she wanted to spring him out of the cells. That manor house in the country must be worth fifty million dollars at least, let alone the grounds of the estate. Everything and everyone had tried to pull her away from her own humble base as a straightforward cop. She'd been tricked into acting like a crook herself. She was a bodyguard, a cheap throwaway. People with infinite wealth were running the show and she was no more than a pawn. She had to go back to her roots. She had to stay with Randolph. She loved the wealth and adventure. She needed to surrender and face up to her crimes. Her position was so contradictory that no compromise was possible. She'd drawn a red line. That alone would decide her fate, or she wanted to believe so.

His pull on her was so strong both on her body and her emotions. She'd put him behind bars once. Could she ever do it again?

His strong protective arm was around her shoulders, her arm around his waist feeling the tight flex of his muscles as he moved. Maybe she could do her duty for the sake of law and order and betray him? For sure she could, after they'd made love enough to last the rest of her life.

Chapter 22

She woke at 4:30 a.m. In the distance on Via Torino the trams had started their dawn chorus of squealing steel. How far from home she was. Randolph was sleeping contentedly on his back, his hand on her thigh. She ran her fingers across his sculpted abdomen. His hard erect penis jutted upwards reaching his navel. She folded her hand around, kneading the unyielding flesh. In the half light she could see his features as she began to masturbate him. A smile grew on his lips, parting them into a deep voiced sigh, building to a groan. She increased her grip and her speed. She just wanted him to come, wanted him helpless as she watched him. He was beginning to wake.

"That's so good."

"I'm not going to stop until you come. You're a bad boy lying there with an enormous dick wanting to shoot it all out. I know you were having sexy thoughts."

"I've been rock hard ever since that shower. I was thinking of your soft pussy. I was thinking of you coming in your hot wet pussy and you letting go like that. I was thinking of your wet panties, pulling them aside and kissing your juice ... God, Kaitlyn."

She slowed and synced to his convulsions of ecstasy as his sperm jetted onto his hard rippled belly and ran down onto her hand. He opened his eyes.

"You make me feel wanton and naughty too."

She lay back, pulled off the bed cover and took some of his cum on her fingers. She ran her hand into her groove.

"You've made me so wet, I've got to come. Do you mind? Am I being a bad girl?"

"Hell, you're making me want to come again."

She began a slow delicious masturbation, watching his eyes follow her hand.

"My lonely days often began this way. I've got a little buzz friend at home to help me. I'm thinking of all that cum squirting out of your cock, thinking of you inside me, coming in my pussy, holding me tight with your hard cock."

She could smell his semen and her own juice. His body had become musky. She was close, circling her own stiff little shaft, holding herself, holding herself tight. He was kneeling over her, jerking off his cock again.

"You're so wet. I love that juicy pussy sound. You're making me come again."

The wave broke and cascaded through her body as he pulsed out his seed again onto her breasts.

"I'm doing it on you, come in your wet pussy angel. I can't stop," he growled."

She looked up at his head tilted back as he helplessly worked the aftershocks of ejaculation with his strong hand. His tremors of pleasure oozed onto her belly as she kept her fingers tight against her clitoris in the resolution of her own orgasm.

"I just had to be a naughty girl, my lover man."

"Never ever hold back for me. I could come just thinking about you," he said with his normal warm smile.

"Are we bad, bad people?"

"I love you, Kaitlyn."

"I love you, Randolph."

They took a slow late breakfast in their room. Randolph made a couple of calls on the hotel phone. Within a few minutes a delivery guy arrived with a laptop computer and a cheap cellphone. Once he got connected to the wifi he brought a screen squirming with red and green numbers.

"Do you want to make your first million, sugar?" he asked.

He was seated on the foot of the bed wearing a body-hugging white T-shirt and Armani ripped jeans, his tanned thigh teasing and tempting through the gaps.

"I wish. How the hell am I going to do that?"

"You look for market volatility. I'm looking at the value of the British pound against the Euro. The prime minister is going to make a speech later in Florence about Britain leaving the European Union. The markets are nervous and selling pounds. My guess is her speech will sound optimistic about the economy and the pound will go back up. Do you agree?"

"Sure, you're a billionaire banker, I'm a poor cop so how could I disagree?"

"So you've made an investment decision and I believe it's a winner."

"One problem my hunky honey money monkey is that I don't have any cash."

He laughed.

"Hey, I'm sure going to get that put on my business cards. Randolph Quinn: Hunky honey money monkey. OK, first day of your MBA degree. What can you do when you've got no cash?"

"Get a loan, steal, walk the streets selling my physical assets?"

"OK, you've passed the Sackman-Platinum security, business plan, and character checks. Clearly you've grasped the business. We're giving you 20 million US dollars to play with."

Her eyes widened.

"How could I repay it?"

"We'll charge you ten thousand dollars to borrow that cash for about an hour and we're trying to get you a million."

"But I might lose it."

"Trust me."

"You keep saying that."

"You're borrowing my money and now you're borrowing my lines."

He tapped on the keys.

"So, here's your trading account in your name and I've just deposited a loan of twenty million dollars. Take a look."

She stared over his shoulder at the screen. A Sackman-Platinum bank account statement showed the balance in her name.

"You're actually frightening me, Randolph. I can't risk like this."

"That's the difference between the winner and the loser. Risk is just the loser's word for low self-esteem."

"You sure aren't a loser on that basis."

"The pound is still sliding against the euro and the US dollar. We've got a couple of the news channels we own pumping out fear and doom about her speech. When the value reaches the floor you're going to push a key on here and buy. Keep an eye on that red flashing number. When it stops flashing the Sackman-Platinum algorithm is looking ahead of people's trading positions and telling me we're as low as we're going to go."

"And then?"

"If you'd bought already you would have lost about four million dollars on paper."

"Fucking hell."

"You see, the number is stable. People have stopped selling but the market won't know it for about four seconds. We buy at the cheapest price. Do you trust me to make you a rich woman?"

"Oh God, yes, yes of course. Are you really, really serious that I could be a millionaire or broke?"

He tapped a few keys and then brought up another screen.

"I'm playing my own ninety million on the same deal. I'm buying with South African rand and I'll probably sell into Malaysian ringgits. That's just me being greedy to exploit a couple of small shivers in the market."

"So have I bought British pounds and lost myself four million dollars?"

"You will have when you push my shift key here."

She dried the sweat from her palms, reached over and tapped the key.

"So what do we do now?"

"I'll keep half an eye to the figures and sort out my schedule for the day. I came here for a business meeting remember and that's far more important than this little sideshow. She felt like pacing the room but to him this was just a bit of small change.

He picked up the new cellphone and made a call.

"Giorgi, what do you know, my man?"

She could hear the other man's voice but he was speaking in Italian. Randolph nodded seriously.

"That's Chinatown right? Have we cleared it with the Fuk Lo Fat? Good, good. I'll be with you half past noon. Love you man."

Her head was spinning. While Randolph had been speaking on the phone, the red figure had turned to green. The value was climbing and climbing. He glanced at the figures.

"About now our news channels are putting on the painted face money girls reporting that it's looking good for the value of the pound. That'll be enough to get the schmucks piling in to buy. Once they start the price will come right up and at the top we sell to all those wide-mouthed greedy goldfish gulping for gold at the surface."

"Not that you're greedy of course."

"We're beyond greed, my lovely woman. We are the world. We are everything. Greed is for those who think there's still more and more. We know what there is and we've got it covered. The super rich need two simple things in order to keep their position."

"And they are?"

"The uneducated poor and the educated greedy. Our world systems of education and opportunity do their best to keep things that way."

"You really should be a professor of economics."

"When we cash in your little deal in a minute you can think of buying me that little cottage and an old-fashioned pedal bike. Then I could be your quirky old stay-at-home academic.

She sighed.

"I would give a million for that Randolph. I bloody well would."

He reached out and gently caressed her cheek.

"I know you would and I love you for that."

"But it could never be, could it?"

"When I'm rich I'll consider it."

"You're a jerk."

His eyes were now quick and keen as he concentrated on the screen.

"We're at the top, sugar. The schmucks still want to buy but there's no one selling. Our little wedge of cash will feed the frenzy and also push the price down. We can sell at the top price four seconds before they know they're losers. Hit the space bar, big shot banker."

He took her finger and tapped the keyboard. For about four seconds the number stayed green. Then it went to red and then flashing red.

"What happened?"

"Ummmm, looks like you made one million eight hundred thousand US dollars."

"What's that in British pounds?"

He thought for about half a second.

"It's trading at point seven five. That's one million three hundred and fifty thousand pounds."

"Bloody hell."

He was tapping again.

"So, I've clawed back the ten thousand as interest on the loan and we're done."

"And what did you make?"

"There was a bit of a hitch and I had to take a small reduction but I've made enough to get us dinner tonight."

"How much Randolph?"

"Seven and a quarter million dollars."

"For a few minutes work?"

"For a few minutes work based on inside information on the contents of the speech, TV news channels owned by the bank and a laser trading system that puts us ahead of the market."

She knew she should be appalled. These guys didn't work or make anything. They didn't give a damn for society or human lives. They skimmed the cream every minute of every day while the world toiled for crusts. She was rich. And she loved the feeling. To enjoy it she had to be alive and not in jail.

"So what's the action in Chinatown?"

"That's where I'm meeting our good Albanian godfather, Valmir Rudovic. He's not such a bad old boy after all."

"Really?"

"His account just loaned you twenty million. I just thought it would be nice if he made up for all the trouble he's caused us."

She laughed.

"You're a bastard, an absolute bastard."

"That's what they pay me for, ma'am."

"That means I've given ten thousand dollars of my hard earned cash as interest to a hood who wants to wipe us out."

"Not quite. Sackman-Platinum took that as a handling fee. The dealing helps to legitimize his dirty account. He should be grateful. I might even slap on a transaction charge."

She shook her head. He had both the cheek and the dick of the devil."

"So, how do I get this cash? I'll need something to pay off my pathetic little credit card."

"We can transfer a small amount but too much will alert the tax man. I'll move twenty thousand, OK?"

"Sure. How can this be real?"

"Kaitlyn, I ask myself that question every day. Give me your account details."

She was rich. She was rich. She was fucking greedy selfish ecstatic rich. She was more than a millionaire. She took a deep breath. To Randolph this was just an idle morning. The most frightening thing in her own mind was her sense of pleasure and happiness.

"Let's get down to business. How do you fancy a Chinese meal later?"

"Crispy duck, pancakes, chilli beef?"

"You got it."

She decided to dress down. She chose a Prada brown leather bomber jacket, a white Gucci ruffled georgette silk blouse, Prada black flared denim pants and the patent leather boots.

"You look hyper-unbelievable fantastic," he said.

"I feel like a million dollars."

"You look like twenty-five million."

"You'll have to let me tap on your screen again."

"No worries. Let's be serious for a minute. I want you to be armed, and believe me, I'm not thinking of anyone getting shot. If we're armed it means we don't get a fight. *Capisce?*"

"Armed with what?"

He went to the holdall and pulled out a shoulder holster containing a Glock 26 snub nose pistol.

"I know this is your favourite. It's loaded and I've got plenty of ammo."

"You think of everything."

She was thinking hard. She had drawn a red line and if she had salvaged anything of her own soul that had to mean something. The money, the lifestyle, the power had seduced her, she admitted that to herself. That was why the red line had to be red.

"No more killing."

"Nothing we're going to do."

Her heart was pounding. Just wearing this fearsome gun in a public place was enough to put her in an Italian prison for a few years. He was her man and she had lost her heart to him, but an honest police officer had no soul on offer.

They boarded a tram. A few older women sat like bemused peasants at a fabulous fashion catwalk show. Every girl was a model, every male was a peacock. As she'd left the hotel she'd felt overdressed. On this humble tram she felt a little off the pace. They swayed, rattled and screeched their way across this beautiful city. Again she saw the cathedral and La Scala opera theater. They passed the park Sempione where she'd dumped the truck. Randolph had chosen a mid-blue Versace double-breasted business suit, a slim red tie and black brogue shoes. He kept her hand in his, holding her eyes for long delicious minutes. The overhead sign read the name of the next stop Piazza Antonio Baiamonti.

"This is where we get off."

Her own heart was pounding. Her mouth was dry. She could feel Randolph's tension and if he was tense, then she had every right to be terrified. A short way ahead on a corner was the figure of the guy she'd met yesterday, Giorgi Deez.

He didn't join them but walked on the other side of a small street called Via Paolo Sarpi. A small Chinese guy wobbled along the sidewalk with a wheelbarrow piled high with bales of fabric. Every business, restaurant, and shop had Chinese names and characters above their windows.

"Right, our man is above a jeweller's shop. This is Chinatown, not Camorra territory, not Albanian nor Russian. This is a foreign country where Italian police don't enter. This is the land of the Fuk Lo Fat. They're a Chinese Mafia that run the sweat shops that feed the legit fashion business and the fake fashion business. And you'll love this—they're often the same items."

"Why is he here?"

"Valmir Rudovic was stupid enough to introduce a few of his own adolescent slave girls at the upper end of the prostitute racket. That is Fuk Lo Fat work. We asked for their cooperation. These guys are business men and do a lot of deals with Sackman-Platinum. Let's just say we have a mutual interest in this matter."

"So he's not here of his own free will."

"That's for sure. He could have had a quiet executive conference over a superb meal. He wanted to play it rough, but he's a bonehead."

"What now?"

"I'm going to inform him that his unprofessional conduct will mean that the bank will close his account. I want him to understand that any tantrums won't be tolerated."

"And if he doesn't agree."

"Then I'll leave him to the Fuk Lo Fat."

"They'll kill him?"

"They'll make a consensual decision based on their long-term business plan."

"They'll kill him."

"They'll eliminate a strategic risk to their corporate growth profile."

Giorgi had taken up station in a doorway opposite the jeweller's shop. Randolph gave him a wave and opened the door. There was a smell of Chinese spice. A small man signaled them to follow him up creaky unlit stairs. A door swung open into a bare smoke-filled room. Several young men leaned on the flaking walls, cigarettes dangling from their mouths. A muscular bare-chested guy toyed with a large kitchen meat cleaver. A heavy man of about forty was seated on a plastic garden chair. A large wild mustache gave him an oddly comic look. The atmosphere was edgy, ripe with sweat and violence.

"Valmir, my old friend," said Randolph extending a hand.

"Thief. You pig thief," replied the man, standing up.

"You pig rapist and girl snatcher. You pig trader in refugee misery. You pig heroin dealer. You pig rich man thanks to me. You call me pig? You dare to call me pig?"

Without warning Randolph drove his fist into the guy's face. The Chinese boys laughed and shouted to each other in Chinese. Kaitlyn's gut tightened. She'd never seen him like this, never guessed his character. His anger seemed genuine and nothing to do with the grubby business of money.

The big guy stumbled and came forward for a second evading Randolph and facing up to her.

"You bring pig whore with you. I'll fuck her tight asshole."

In a split second she drove a karate blow into his gut. He doubled over with a squeal. The Chinese guys shouted with intense excitement. What the hell was she doing? She'd drawn a red line for Randolph and she'd crossed it herself.

"Valmir. I'm closing your account with Sackman-Platinum. I just can't do business with a man who'd attack my wife," said Randolph.

"Wife?"

"I'm a banker, I rely on predicting the future."

"Fuck. What the fuck?" she gasped.

"Gentlemen—I leave him to you. You know his drug operation in Shanghai. You know the Chinese girls he's using in Paris and New York. You know the teenage girls he's selling cheap to bust your business in Italy. Your move, guys," said Randolph.

The slouching young men pushed away from the walls. The bare-chested man with the cleaver stepped forward and grabbed the Albanian by the hair. Kaitlyn knew this was going to be ugly.

The noise of the street stuttered up the stairs. She caught the sound of a screaming vehicle engine and the crack of gunfire. She led the way down to the street. The Fiat van was back. A guy was down on the sidewalk, blood trickling toward the gutter. She focused on the open end of a gun barrel pointed toward her. She responded as trained, pulling her gun. A robot taking the stance, lining up the target into the main body mass, looking down the sights. Shoot to be sure. Shoot to win. Shoot to kill.

"Armed police. Drop the weapon."

Even as she said the words she realized she wasn't a cop in Milan. She was in a shootout with rival gangsters. Four rounds thumped into the heart and lungs of her opponent, smoking and sending fragments of cloth spinning from his jacket. He dropped. Final. No way back. Dead.

Randolph was storing his Walther PPK. Now three bodies lay in the street. A gang of young Chinese men dragged each corpse back into the Fiat van. Then they boarded themselves and the vehicle moved off slowly towards the intersection and the bustle of horn-blasting Milan traffic. A toothless old man threw a bucket of water over the blood and pushed it into the gutter with a broom. Another guy trotted by with a barrow loaded with bales of fabric, a black Mercedes cruised up the street, a young woman swerved around pedestrians ringing the bell of her bicycle. Life closed in around the wound. Healed. Sealed. Deal done.

She began to walk, Randolph at her side. The gun was warm against her chest. She was breathing hard.

"That was a fucking bloodbath, a fucking disaster," she said.

"Those boys were stupid coming in to Chinatown. With Albanians it's all about what they call the Fis, the clan. They're kind of like bees stinging and dying to save their hive. They take an oath; they call it Besa and they can't escape it. They had to die to keep the honor of their families. From our point of view our customer service complaint has been resolved and Sackman-Platinum has scooped twenty-nine billion dollars. After all, that money doesn't exist."

"The Chinese didn't kill them, we did."

"Doesn't always pay to be too technical."

"We killed three men."

"We killed one each. Giorgi must have got the first one."

"Where is he?"

They arrived at the junction with Via Giovanni Battista Niccolini. A red Ferrari GT4 Lusso pulled up with Giorgi Deez grinning behind the wheel. Randolph opened the door. Kaitlyn scrambled into the back.

"There's bound to be police here any minute," she said.

"Why should there be?"

"Don't be stupid, you know why."

"The Chinese Triads are the cops. No one calls the police if they want to stay alive. You got a problem you see the Fuk Lo Fat," said Giorgi.

The Ferrari accelerated away. Randolph gave Giorgi's shoulder a playful punch.

"What happened to you?"

"I dropped the first guy as he got out of the van. I saw you come out of that shop into my field of fire. You were on top of the job so I slipped through a barber's shop, picked up the car so I could show it off and give you a ride."

Kaitlyn had to admire his sang froid. The biggest danger with police shootouts is crossfire. Yes, Randolph had been right; he was a battle-hardened pro. They pulled up in Via Medici.

"That's all folks. I leave you young lovers in peace."

Even as Kaitlyn got out of the car she knew it was over. The red line she'd drawn was soaked in blood. How much she wanted to cling to him for reassurance and protection. There could never be any future with him. Even if this time they'd beaten off an Albanian clan, the next time it would be the Russian mob, the Chinese Triads or the good old-fashioned New York Mafia. It would never, ever, ever end.

She held his hand, still in love with him as a man, even more revolted by his life. They took the hotel elevator in silence. Once in the room she stripped off the gun and slumped onto the bed. Her tears were something of a relief.

"I warned you, Randolph. I told you I wouldn't accept any more death or violence. You can't expect me to be part of this. I'm a cop for Christ's sake. I've sworn an oath to Her Majesty the Queen to uphold the law and protect all people from harm. I can't live as a criminal and killer."

He sat down and gently massaged her back. The sensation was seductive, delicious. She loved him. She loved him.

"I don't want you as an unwilling partner. You've pulled off some brilliant work."

"This isn't work. Police work is telling the truth, the preservation of life and morality."

"What about the poor cows who work as prostitutes for Valmir Rudovic? They select poor kids from villages. They rape them, often get them hooked on drugs. They sell them on to other pimps who rape them again and again. How are the police getting on with stopping all that?"

"You don't stop them either. You just get fat on their dirty business."

"There's more to it than that."

"Tell me what."

"I can't do that, not here not today. I can't. Let's just say I've disrupted their business model today."

"It's always *mañana*. I'm not going to be led along just because of my personal feelings for you. Decency and honesty are bigger than my own ridiculous desires."

"You're a good person, Kaitlyn. A good person also knows the value of trust and that's all I'm asking."

"I trusted you today not to start killing again."

"OK officer, list our choices as we came out into the street back there. We've got two thugs pointing guns at us. Maybe they were making a gangster movie and we got it all wrong. I never asked you to pull your weapon. You could have just died to prove your faith in truth and morality."

"But you created the situation. You went there. You know damn well that those Chinese guys are going to execute your Valmir Rudovic."

"It's their choice. No one tells the Fuk Lo Fat how to run their show."

"I can't live with this. Whatever I feel, whatever I want for myself can't happen when all this stuff is in my mind. This is over, Randolph. Over."

For a while he didn't reply but stroked her back and hair. She didn't dare to turn toward him and see his face and his eyes.

"So what will you do?"

"Get to an airport, get a plane to London and then just hand myself in I suppose."

"Do you think they'll want you? I'm not going to hold you prisoner. I understand everything you're saying to me."

"I'll give you back all that money as soon as I can sort out my bank."

"That money is yours. Don't give it to me because it's not mine, never was mine. Sackman-Platinum gave you a loan and some investment advice. You took that risk and you took that risk because you trusted me. Are you telling me you trust me with your money but can't trust me as a man?"

"Probably yes, Randolph. You're trying to slime your way through my conflicted feelings, but that's the shape of it."

"If you can't trust me now you should go, you have to go."

He stopped stroking her back. His tone had grown hard and cold. It was as if the sun had gone out. Perhaps in her heart she had hoped that some fairy godmother would descend and make everything good again. It was better to lie here not looking at him, telling him that it was over than to stand up, actually stand up, look into his eyes and finish it forever.

"Yes, yes, I should go."

"I'll get you a cab. Take everything in that suitcase. Once you're gone I don't want to be finding any memories of you."

She got up, threw everything carelessly into the Louis Vuitton suitcase and snapped it shut.

"I've got no passport. It was in my case in the back of that car we crashed."

"I'll fix it."

"How can you fix it?"

"Trust me, but of course you don't, do you?"

She winced at the bitterness in his voice. She wanted to reach out to him, tell him that she hadn't meant it, not meant it to be hurtful, because, because she was in love with him. She had to get away, run away from this eight-legged spider of conflict that was chasing her. She flashed her mind back to her old life of a girls' night karaoke, Bingo with her mum, the karate club, a bottle of wine and a movie with Camille. More likely she'd be sitting in jail. She could stop this now by reaching out for his hand, kissing his lips, letting her soul melt into him and forget everything in the world except his touch and her feeling of safety in his hard fearless arms.

"Randolph, I chose to be a cop, and that choice was my last. From then on you do what's honest. There *is* good and bad and those bookends will always be at either end of the books of life no matter what books you buy and sell to put on your shelf. There *is* good and bad."

"And one of the worst things is not to trust."

"You're playing with what I'm saying. Believe me I want you to defeat my argument, convince me to stay. There is good and bad. There is right and wrong."

He turned away from her and called a taxi.

"Four minutes downstairs. There's an Al Italia flight AZ 238 to London Gatwick at five o'clock. When you get to the ticket desk there'll be a boarding pass for you and a paper to show to the passport control."

"How?"

"I'll fix it while you're traveling. Sackman-Platinum can fix anything."

"Look, thanks. Randolph please, don't be so cold. I...."

"Without trust there's fuck all, Kaitlyn. You know how I felt about you and you've made your choice not to trust me. Your cab will be here."

He turned back to the window overlooking the street and didn't look round. She could just run to him now, put her arms around him one last time, one last time. She snatched up the bag, opened the door and went to the elevator. The cab was waiting. She took a last look up at the room. She could call out to him. Call out that she loved him. Her eyes searched the bare window. Good or bad, right or wrong, he was gone.

Chapter 23

She closed her eyes in the back of the taxi. Would anyone ever believe what had happened to her? She called Camille.

"It can't be you. I've just put the phone down from talking to your boss Shannon Knightsmith and now you pop up," said Camille.

"What did she want?"

"She made me promise to tell her at once if I heard from you."

"Did she say why?"

"Scotland Yard squad commanders who happen to be aristocrats don't share their complex motives with simple souls like me."

"As far as you know, am I any sort of wanted list?"

"Of course not."

"Can you run a check?"

She heard Camille tapping her keyboard.

"Nope."

"No Interpol red notice arrest warrants from France or Italy?"

"No, have you been on the booze?"

"I wish. Are you going to tell Shannon I called?"

"I'm a foot soldier, she's a big boss so I guess I'd do as I'm told unless there's some serious reason you need a favor as a friend."

"No, that's fine. I'm flying back from Milan tonight."

"Did they pull you out?"

"No, I've walked out."

"Is that what Scotland Yard wants you to do?"

"Who knows, but I can't live with it. It's too difficult to explain."

"And what about on the intimate front my dear?"

"We had a thing but it's over."

"Did you tell him?"

"Sure."

"Did you remember to tell yourself?"

"Of course."

"So you're coming back to zoom around in your big car or on your motorbike and do speeding tickets for the rest of your career?"

"Right now that's sounds like heaven. We'll catch up as soon as I'm back. Love you."

The taxi had hit the freeway back to Malpensa airport. It was good news that she was not on a wanted list, at least she wouldn't be arrested at London Heathrow. She closed her eyes again wanting to think about how she would handle the business of handing herself in. Her crimes had been committed abroad so she could anticipate imprisonment in France or Italy. She would have no friends or contacts. Her mind slipped ridiculously to Randolph, how it felt to kiss him, to touch him, to feel him inside her. Her cellphone was ringing. She checked the screen. It was DCI Shannon Knightsmith. She let it ring and ring. In desperation she answered.

"Yes?"

"Kaitlyn, what the hell are you doing?"

"I'm coming home. I'm going to hand myself in. I can't live like this."

"Live like what?"

"Like a crook. Like a killer. Like a thief."

"OK, keep calm. You've done well. Get back to England and don't worry. Now listen carefully. Do not and I mean *do not* speak to anyone about where you have been or anything that happened. No one is going to arrest you. No one in London is interested in anything that's happened. No one in the world is crying about any of the vermin you've dealt with. You're an honest cop. You've got integrity and a sense of justice. I've spoken to Randolph and he adores you for that."

"What? You've spoken to him? You've talked to him about me? He tells you his feelings about me?"

"Sometimes a man wants to talk. They're not all emotionally retarded."

"This is crazy. I'm the cop. He's the crook, killer or psychopath and my boss is chatting with him about my character."

"Never miss the chance to listen to anyone, especially crooks."

Kaitlyn let out a long sigh. She couldn't deny the sense of the advice, and the methods of top detectives were way beyond her. It still stung her that she'd been talking to Randolph about her.

"So I report for work on traffic patrol tomorrow morning?"

"I'll let you know about that quite soon. Remember, nothing has happened. No one cares. No one and I mean no one needs to know. That's an order and you ignore it at your absolute peril."

"Ciao," said Kaitlyn as she clicked off. What the hell was that about? Randolph had spoken to her. She almost gathered that he'd phoned her. She knew that Randolph was a business associate of Shannon's husband. She knew that Randolph had been to their stately home. Somehow all these dead bodies, gunfights, missiles, grenades and machine guns were of no interest to the forces of law and order. If that were so, was there any point in believing in law and order? A few days ago she'd been pondering if Shannon and her husband were rich crooks like Randolph. Maybe she should forget her advice and trust in good old-fashioned police integrity and hand herself in?

The taxi pulled in at Terminal 2. She handed over her credit card.

"*E pagato gia,* paid. The bank pay," said the driver.

She thanked him. Infinite wealth, infinite ease, everything at the wave of a hand. Money solved everything; no wonder everybody wanted it.

She made her way to the Al Italia desk. A beautiful dark-eyed olive-skinned girl beamed a professional smile.

"Signora Thorn, please we show you to the first class lounge. What would you like to drink?"

"Are you sure you've got the right person?"

"*Si,* you are Sackman-Platinum yes?"

"Yes. Did they explain I've lost my passport?"

"*Si certo,* it is all done. Your security and immigration is all complete."

She shrugged. How seductive is wealth. Can anyone resist its power and once you've tasted it wouldn't you always crave it?"

"Did you choose a drink?"

"Gin and tonic please, a double."

143

"*Certo.* The computer area is here if you wish to work. The terminals are all secure."

She had over an hour before boarding. She sat down and brought up her e-mails. As usual nearly everything was junk. There was a message from Sackman-Platinum welcoming her and showing her account balance of one million, eight hundred thousand dollars. She needed to give an address where she could receive her debit card. She brought up her normal UK account. The balance was about forty pounds under twenty thousand. She'd gone two pounds overdrawn and her bank had charged her forty pounds. How she loved bankers. But, there was her twenty thousand Randolph had transferred. She checked her credit card. All cleared and paid. This was the first time in her life she'd been solvent let alone rich. She just couldn't accept all this, but she couldn't deny the pleasure at not having to fret about debt and the rent.

She checked her Facebook page. Several friends were pulling silly immature faces from a mountain top in Spain, one had a fabulous new job, one was bragging about her new car and house. She sipped the gin and tonic wondering if she should update the world with her own little adventures. She thought back to Shannon's warning. No; there was something in her tone which had chilled her. She risked another gin and tonic. Every time she didn't have a focus her mind flipped back to Randolph. She hadn't known him long but hell, she'd known him strong. He was generous, considerate, a sexy, sexy rock hard but gentle lover. He was gorgeous to look at, courageous, and decisive. He had uncountable wealth. Then there was the violence and the cold-hearted indifference toward an enemy. In every corner of her mind it was over. In every corner of her heart she'd never even started to give him the love she held in reserve for the right man. Perhaps she could let her heart run free, still in love with him until the end of time. She didn't have to stop that feeling as long as it didn't spread to her head. Soon enough one of the endless girls who gazed at him would catch his eye and she would have him, touch him, feel him move inside her. A tidal wave of anger pulsed through her, making her grind her teeth. The plane was boarding. She thought back to the last time she'd been at 38,000 feet. Oh Randolph, fuck you, Randolph Quinn.

As the Airbus A320 taxied in to Terminal Two at London Heathrow airport she realized that still no firm plan had formed in her mind. Her boss Shannon had told her to do nothing, say nothing. Did she trust her? Was she being given orders merely to cover up some collusion or corruption involving Sackman-Platinum and people above her in the police? She'd always been a good girl, owned up, done the decent thing. How could that suddenly be wrong? And yes, she was a millionaire and then some. And yes, she was in love with a killer. She needed advice and needed to talk. In her police work she'd met many lonely people but not until this moment had she understood the terrible deafness of loneliness at the concert of life. At least being alone meant there was no one else to interfere with her decision. Once she had reclaimed her suitcase she would act and there could be no going back. She stood by the carousel as the cases began to appear. Soon most of them had been claimed and finally there was nothing. She stared at the empty moving conveyor until it stopped. It wasn't the end of the world if the bag had been lost or was on its way to Timbuktu but it was a hassle she could do without. All the case contained was half a year's police salary in fashion clothes. She looked around for an airport official. A woman's voice spoke from behind her.

"It won't be coming. It's been transferred to your next flight."

"What the fuck?"

She turned to look into the beautiful face of Detective Inspector Shannon Knightsmith who reached out to touch her arm.

"What are you doing to me?"

"Nothing bad, I promise you that."

"Let me go. You're my boss, but I'm a free person. I don't want to get on any other plane. I don't trust you. I don't know what you're up to but you've got some connection to that bank and Randolph and you don't want me to spill the beans."

Shannon smiled and nodded.

"You know that's a pretty good analysis all in all. We're at a crossroads here aren't we?"

"Yeah, and I've chosen the honest straightforward road. I've done wrong but I'll be honest with you. I suspect you're not on the level. Scotland Yard detectives don't shrug off

145

killings and they sure don't talk to a crook about one of their own officers. I don't care what bloody rank you are, Shannon. I'm going to hand myself in and tell the whole truth."

"You're not. If you had any idea what powers there are to stop you doing that, you'd be terrified, believe me. If by any chance you did anything so stupid you'd be executed. I admire your strength and integrity. We need to be friends and we will be."

"But you'd have me executed?"

"Not just you, any operator who compromised our business."

For a moment Kaitlyn felt tearful, frightened, confused. Randolph had let slip the term *operator* a couple of times. She wasn't going to back down. Right and wrong existed in the human soul and she wouldn't ever deny it for a pocket full of gold. She wanted to get onto the front foot.

"What do you mean *our business*? Our business is the Metropolitan police."

"I'm talking about Sackman-Platinum."

"You can't be serious. They're money launderers, mercenaries. They're no better than the Mafia."

"But they're mightier than the Mafia, Kaitlyn, and in this business might is right. Listen, your case is already loaded onto our plane. As soon as we're aboard we will be flying to New York. You have nothing to fear and you have no choice."

"Of course I've got a choice. This is London, England, a civilized country where there's rule of law. You can fuck right off."

"Randolph was just so right about you from the first moment. You're courageous and straight. I must admit he also noticed your beauty but he's a man so he's not always totally competent and professional."

"Are you two in some kind of relationship?"

Shannon laughed.

"I think my husband would kill him."

"I'm going to walk away from you and this is all over for me, Shannon. I'm sorry but I will not go deeper and deeper into this *business* as you put it."

"Take a look around at the exits."

Kaitlyn looked around the baggage hall. Men or women who looked like cops stood at every door. Her legs felt weak, her mouth dry.

"Shannon, please. As a woman, please let me go."

"I've ordered British beer-battered fish and chips for my inflight meal. Do you fancy the same with a bottle of Chablis?"

This was surreal. She was effectively being kidnapped by her boss and discussing fish and chips. Kaitlyn found herself laughing more or less in panic. She held out her hands in surrender. Play dead. Play for time.

"I'm not sure if I've ever had Chablis?"

"I'm not sure myself but I saw it on the menu. My husband's a right old wine snob so I stay deliberately ignorant to annoy him and to let him big himself up all at once."

"He's the guy who's a commodity dealer and the Earl of Bloxington?"

"That's my hugga bear Spencer."

This banal chat had calmed her, brought her breathing under control. If she got a chance she'd run, but for now she'd act as normal as possible.

"Shannon, is it a really dumb question to ask why we're flying to New York?"

"It's a semi-dumb question because it's taken you a while to relax enough to ask it. Now you've dropped all that, you can start to feel excited."

"How so?"

"'cause that's where the Sackman-Platinum trading center is; Hudson River Exchange. We're 52 stories of platinum-plated wealth looking right back at Manhattan but with our feet in Jersey City."

"Yeah, but why am I going there?"

"Randolph tells me you're a recent wealthy client and I'm telling you I want you completely away from the Metropolitan police. Let me square with you. We selected you and used you before we had the chance to tell you everything you had a right to know. I can't tell you much because I'm a foot soldier like you and it's not my place to act the big shot. Come on, let's get on board."

The platinum-liveried jet was a short bus ride from the terminal. She glanced at the plane.

"That's not the same one that I took to Milan."

"No, we've got a few. Randolph's still got that one in Italy. He's an old-fashioned Englishman who has to go upstairs to bed."

Kaitlyn felt a surge of jealousy and anger. Maybe he'd already taken the stairs with his next unwitting assistant assassin. The plane audio system distracted her.

"This is Captain Cameron McDonald. Welcome on board our Boeing 787 Dreamliner. We have priority clearance for takeoff. Weather is good all across the pond. Looking to land JFK at about 7 p.m. local time."

She glanced down the interior of the cabin. The whole place was set up as a grand salon with a rich carpeted floor, leather chairs, and sofas. There was a central fountain with platinum spouting goldfish and cherubs. A white grand piano was in the distance. Kaitlyn blinked at the sight.

Shannon caught the direction of her eyes.

"The boss likes to play. It helps her think. This is her personal plane."

"That's Stella Boursellino?"

"Yeah, you saved her life in Paris. Believe me, Kaitlyn, you'll never be poor and you'll never walk alone."

"It's tragic I guess, to fall from her horse so young."

Shannon fixed her eyes on Kaitlyn.

"You're in too deep to pull out of this show, so I'm going to tell you one thing. Stella didn't fall from a horse. That's the PR stuff for the mags and the daytime TV. She was an NYPD officer. She stopped a bullet. She was an educated high-flyer headed for the top. She got a payout and the proceeds of a charity ball. She could have sat out the rest of her life. She studied the markets and played every cent. She got rich and then she got richer."

"Did she start Sackman-Platinum?"

"That's another story and she'll tell you that herself."

Kaitlyn settled into a soft chair. How could she stop herself from rolling in this wealth like a foal rolling joyfully in hay? So Stella had been a cop. For some reason the information comforted her.

"Shannon, are you a straight police officer or what?"

"Sure. At the start of this business I knew a little. I was called in when you arrested Randolph but I had met him

148

socially before. He came down to the estate to meet a couple of minor royals when they were weekend guests. You'd be surprised how many people want to meet the world's wealthiest and best-looking man. I bet he's never told you that he handles the Queen's accounts personally? The witness protection stuff was a little scam I had to pull to get him out of jail. At that moment I was doing what some very important people asked me to do. I trusted them and I did it. My husband runs an American operation and banks with Sackman-Platinum. He leases a floor in their Manhattan building."

"So what the fuck is Randolph? Is he James Bond? Is he a banker?"

"He's the richest man in the world. You've seen him work. He's hyper-smart. He figured out accelerated laser trading. The trading commands are wrapped around a permanent clear pulsing beam. The laser interacts with the electrical polarity of the signal and accelerates it beyond the speed of light. He trades in a time that doesn't yet exist. He's a clever guy."

"So other folk can figure this out too?"

"He holds all the patents and all the rights to all business that might use his system in the future."

"That is impressive. It makes all this other stuff even more crazy. Does he have live gunfights with the Albanian Mafia as a hobby because he didn't get an Xbox for Christmas?"

"Next time you see him you can ask him."

"I've no plans for that."

"Did you plan to be here?"

"Huh, no."

"He asked for you. Right or wrong, I fixed you up."

"Like you thought I'd enjoy a bit of murder and maybe I'd steal a truck if things got a bit slow."

"Like you wouldn't mind getting rich and falling in love with a guy who'd fallen for you at first sight. How often does that happen? Perhaps I didn't want you to spend years of your life hiding round a bend some place with a speed gun. Perhaps I was wrong to encourage you to accompany the most exciting and eligible man in the world?"

Kaitlyn sighed. None of these people were normal. It must have been like this for Alice in Wonderland.

"I do see that point, Shannon."

"And you did fall for him?"

"Of course. He's got the whole list. Now I'm a bit worried he might be a techie geek as well."

"So you do think you might see him?"

"I do think, Shannon, that I've very little sway over anything that happens to me."

"Would you care for dinner?" asked a steward in a platinum gray uniform.

They walked through the plane to a walnut-paneled dining room. The table was a dark wood with a huge inlaid Sackman-Platinum crest of a vulture holding a roll of banknotes in its claws. As the plane reached mid-Atlantic, Kaitlyn let go of all thoughts except the delicious fried fish and chips. She sipped the chilled white wine.

"A cheeky little fellow with a mysterious hint of old leather," said Shannon with a laugh.

"I had a boyfriend at university who took me to a wine tasting. That's the sort of stuff he used to say. To me it's fresh pale and interesting like Harry Potter with an erection."

Shannon laughed again.

"I'll tell Spencer that one. He'll think I've been taking lessons."

Kaitlyn smiled and accepted an espresso coffee served with a glass of cognac. Hand herself in for righteous punishment? Had she ever truly meant to? No, the moment had passed and was slipping away deeper and deeper into the warm brandy.

Chapter 24

Sitting in the back of the inevitably platinum-colored Lincoln town car, she was almost too exhausted to take in the sights as they cruised across Brooklyn Bridge and on into Lower Manhattan. It was only 8 p.m. New York time, but it was 2 a.m. in Milan where she had started her day. They drew up under the portico of a massive skyscraper.

"Platinum Tower. The trading center is across the river in Jersey but this place is the prestige office, the executive suites and of course the penthouses," said Shannon.

"Of course, there's bound to be penthouses. Where's Trump Tower?"

"It's way below the height you'll be at. This place is seventy-two stories."

The door was opened by a uniformed security guard as other guys swarmed to carry cases and shield them from any possible incident. The central atrium seemed to rise almost to infinity while drops of colored water ran down into a pool on fiber-optic threads of gold, silver, and platinum which cascaded like a sunburst from above. A twenty-foot-high corporate statue of the platinum logo vulture grasping the roll of banknotes was mounted on a piece of gold the size of a truck in the center. The effect was awesome but to Kaitlyn's mind, crass and vulgar. Rock guitar wailed and hit you in the chest with bass, a panorama of screens carried pictures of trading rooms labelled US dollars, Japanese yen, UK pounds, euros and every world currency all pulsing to the beat of the music. A huge panel showed a giant waterfall like Niagara Falls. The water had been replaced with gold and platinum coins. The words WEALTH and MONEY splashed up in a rainbow

"My uncle was a fairground guy. He'd have loved this," she said.

"My husband hates it and I agree with him. A lot of Sackman-Platinum clients go for this."

"It's awesome. I mean it's trash, but it's still awesome."

She just didn't know what to say. It was brash and vulgar but all the same brutally honest about what they did. Posh London bankers would call you madam and sir and display old master oil paintings but it was the same business. In a way she loved the integrity of Sackman-Platinum.

"Kaitlyn, please understand how great you've been. Tomorrow the world will seem like a very different place. I do want you to know that I've made a personal assessment of you and I really, really, don't want to be shown as wrong."

"So what life plan have you drawn up for me, Shannon? I've cooperated because I didn't have much of a choice and to be frank I think I would like you and I want to trust you, even though all the evidence is against it."

"In your place I'd be pissed. I'd be fucking boiling mad."

"Don't tempt me. Perhaps I'm just being polite."

"We're going to be meeting Stella Boursellino and a few other guys in the morning. In the meantime there's something you must understand. No one can apply to work for or with this bank. It's like the Freemasons, they choose you. You've gone beyond the point of no return. You know very little but you still know too much. You can never go back."

"That's crazy, of course I can go back."

Kaitlyn felt a surge of anger. Who did these people think they were?

"Sure, you can go back to London, see your friends and your family. Maybe you could be a cop in some way. But Kaitlyn Thorn, humble straight traffic cop can no longer be."

"Did you burn my uniform or what?"

"We'll sell it to a film company for a movie. These bankers suck in every penny."

"You've obviously seen my overdraft charges."

"Bottom line: I'm not locking you in your room. I've got no handcuffs. We all trust you and want you as our friend and colleague. You could walk out of here but I promise you, you will have nowhere to go."

She stared at Shannon's face. Despite her beauty she had ruthless steel in her expression.

"Yeah. *Capito.*"

"You're tired. Get a spa treat, get a drink and sleep. Don't forget to look at the view. Manhattan is spectacular at night.

Oh, by the way you could check your statement. Randolph put you on an Angel account."

"Angel account?"

"Sure, the official name is Wings of Wealth. It means that the bank can trade your capital if they believe they've got a hot deal."

"So you could lose it?"

"No, the bank guarantee no loss. Randolph had a tip that Silicon Mountain were going to make a bid for a small tech company that makes nano microchips. These can be implanted into human brains through the eye to control behavior. You may have made a few dollars."

"Bloody hell, Shannon! I might not want to invest in something like that without knowing at least who's holding the remote control."

"Potentially it could cure mental illness and wipe out crime."

"Or mean that no one wrote poetry, fell in love, or tried a new way to dance."

"You're a romantic rebel, Kaitlyn. That's why Randolph loves you."

Shannon took her arm and led her to the elevator. She could feel the acceleration as they shot up to the penthouse level. Two young women in platinum-colored spa tunics met them as the doors opened into a plush deeply-carpeted lobby with two doors labeled Penthouse Platinum and Penthouse Gold.

"Good evening. We are Emmanuelle and Carissima to assist you," said one of them.

Kaitlyn did a double take toward Shannon. What the hell was this?

"Each suite has a spa and you can get a massage, waxing, or whatever you need. The girls will fix your hair and makeup and prepare your clothes for tomorrow. Carissima always assists me, so I'll leave you with Emmanuelle."

"This is astonishing."

"Kaitlyn, you're rich, you're important. This is normal and if you relax with an open mind it's fantastic."

Shannon raised an eyebrow and gave a small wink. This was off the scale but all the same her legs could do with some attention.

Emmanuelle smiled warmly.

"You've had a long day, madam. Please follow me."

Once again she felt herself seduced by the ease and luxury of this lifestyle. The girl seemed friendly and kind, maybe three or four years younger than herself with a sweet open face, perfectly dyed platinum hair and a compact athletic body.

Shannon gave her a two-cheeked continental kiss and waved good night. Kaitlyn followed Emmanuelle into the Gold suite. Three walls were entirely of glass looking out onto the panorama of New York City. She recognized the Empire State and the roof of the Chrysler building. The spa girl pointed out across the Hudson River to a geometric tower which dwarfed all the other structures.

"That's the trading center. Sackman-Platinum is a wonderful company."

"I'm sorry, Emmanuelle, I'm not used to servants or being pampered. You don't just have to trot out the corporate PR."

"They're so kind to me. Everyone wants to work for them."

She seemed genuine, if a little innocent.

"Is this what you do all the time?"

"Sure, there are clients of the bank who stay and sometimes Mr Quinn."

A harsh thought jabbed at her mind.

"Do you girls massage Mr Quinn?"

Emmanuelle laughed.

"You're very direct, madam."

"Look, fuck off with all this *madam*. I'm Kaitlyn Thorn. I'm a London girl like you're a New York girl. There's no distance between us socially as far as I'm concerned OK."

The girl smiled a little nervously.

"Mr Quinn is a very perfect English gentleman. He likes a shoulder massage and sometimes I trim his hair. There are some clients of the bank who are more demanding."

"I can imagine."

"I have bought my own apartment in Manhattan and helped my two sisters through school. My mother needed an operation on her heart, you understand, and Mr Quinn covered it. I love Sackman-Platinum. I'll get you a drink."

"To hell with it. A Jack Daniels—something like a triple with ice please."

Kaitlyn sat down in a soft armchair and gazed out over the city. There didn't seem to be any curtains or blinds. Emmanuelle returned with her drink.

"How do you shut out the light?"

"The glass can be polarized. From the outside it always looks like a mirror but you can always see out if you want to. Watch."

She went to a wall switch and operated a controller. The view disappeared and the glass wall became dark. This was impossible. Kaitlyn shook her head. These guys had planes, a luxury liner, cars, buildings all around the world, helicopters, and on, and on and on. Without thinking she spoke aloud to herself."

"How many fucking poor bastards in the world slave all their lives and die with fucking nothing?"

"No one has ever asked that question in here," Emmanuelle answered.

She wanted to tell the girl that she was a street cop, struggling to pay her rent, picking up runaway kids whose parents had a drug or gambling habit and no food. She sipped her Jack and let her mind slip away. If she kept busy she could just about pull herself out of the dive into thoughts of Randolph. How he felt inside her, how she'd watched his cum jetting out as she'd brought him to helpless climax. She crossed her legs.

"You're very tired. Maybe you would like to use the spa pool while I arrange your clothes. Perhaps you'd like a massage after all that time on the plane?"

She led her through to a tiled room with red marble scrolls unfurling down into the floor to form a deep pool. The view was still of the city so that she could lie naked in the warm foaming bath as if flying over New York. She stripped and committed herself to total abandon of the mind and soul. The jets of water kneaded her body as she took another slug of the Jack Daniels. How could anyone not be seduced by this? She thought of him again, didn't even try to resist the memory of his touch as her awareness of the water swirling around her clitoris aroused her. All he had wanted was her trust and if she couldn't trust him then she couldn't trust any of the people around her now. But did she care? Even though she'd lost him just the ache of the loss was better than the life she'd had. He was there again, in front of her with his hard dick, wanting her, wet and glistening with desire for her, longing to push softly into her, to press her hot spot and make her weak with lust for his cum. Feeling him climb to his peak as she shuddered with her own orgasm just as he released his own juice in ecstasy deep into her hot belly. The water was pulsing on her, she was holding herself tight and if she kept holding she'd be at a place where she'd be seeing his cum shooting out onto her breasts and smelling their sex musk. If she kept holding the sensation would let go her restraints and looking out into the magic night her pussy would pulse out her orgasm, if she didn't pull back, if she didn't pull back now, she'd come, oh god; oh god. She wasn't coming in her body. Everything had fused into a roar of joy and abandon. She shuddered out her bliss as she closed her eyes and threw back her head. The swirl of water squeezed out the throb of her spasms. Oh God, Randolph, fuck you Randolph.

Her breathing began to recover. She opened her eyes. Emmanuelle was standing on the edge holding an enormous bouquet of roses. She must have seen her, heard her. She'd brought herself off in front of another woman for Christ's sake.

"I was somewhere else in my mind, I didn't see you...."

"I often get like that in there. I drift away and always end up thinking of my partner for some reason. She works for the bank, too."

Her face had the same smiling openness but her eyes carried a depth of understanding and complicity. She knew and obviously enjoyed the same experience.

"The roses?"

"Yes, they've just been delivered for you. That's why I came in."

Kaitlyn sprung out, untroubled by her nakedness.

"You're perfect," said Emmanuelle. "You're so beautiful."

"Thank you. Look, I hope I didn't embarrass you."

The girl smiled.

"There's a card."

She dried her hands and studied the envelope. It read "*A rose for Miss Thorn.*" She tore it open and read the contents. "*My darling Kaitlyn. You're in my heart and wishing you in my arms. Thinking of you in my lonely bed, remembering your touch. Randolph."*

She took a deep breath and fought to hold back her tears. It was bad enough to have come in front of Emmanuelle without starting to sob. All the same she let her emotion overwhelm her.

"Fucking man. You get one under your skin and you have to scratch that itch. If you manage to stop the itch, you long for it to come back because it was so nice to scratch."

"The flowers are so beautiful, I'll look after them. Lie down on the table and we'll take away all your troubles."

Why not? She went to a massage table spread with a rich warm towel. She rested her hand on her chin looking out at the cityscape. She felt Emmanuelle's touch on her body, her legs and her back, shoulders and neck. This was heaven. Once again she was thinking of Randolph, of him in his lonely bed remembering her touch as he'd said in his card. She couldn't deny the pleasure of anonymous hands pressing her ass and backs of her thighs as she ran through her film clip of Randolph. This was decadent and maybe wicked. Her body felt so good, never wanted this to stop. Emmanuelle urged her to roll over onto her back. She worked on her feet, her calves and fronts of her thighs. She just brushed the edge of her pubic hair as she soothed her belly. She couldn't block the memory of his hard cock inside her. This was shameful, she must be soaking. The hands skirted her breasts and worked the sides of her neck and into her jaw, the lids of her eyes and her cheeks.

"I love your tattoo. Ishtar was a powerful woman."

"You know her?"

"I've seen pictures. My partner studies that kind of stuff. I believe Ishtar could be man or woman."

"I think that's why I wanted her on my arm. Thanks so much. Your poor hands must be exhausted."

"I like my work and sometimes I really love it," she said with her broad open smile."

At last she lay in the bed between, of course, silk platinum-colored sheets. This had been something of a day. Who the hell was she now? What the hell was she now? What were these people going to tell her? She pulled out her arm to study the image of the goddess. A warrior, a leader, a politician, a sexual temptress to man or woman. Why had her image entered her the moment she'd first seen it? What had been in her mind when she'd decided to proclaim herself as somehow embodying the spirit of the goddess? Suddenly she saw that since she'd worn the tattoo she'd changed, had been set free to proclaim all the aspects of herself. She'd been shameless with Randolph. The massage had been heaven but surely not erotic. Surely not. She filed away the naughty thought and let her hand slide down. She'd been so wet thinking of him, been so tense, been so stimulated by the folded petals of the roses, soft curled lips, soft wet lips, such a velvet pleasure to touch, you could never stop once you had that itch and the little female shaft was needing to release, like Randolph bursting to jet out his cum from his big thick hard cock as her hand felt the warmth of his pouring seed. She arched her back, longing for her fingers to be his tongue. Fuck, do it in me Randolph. Do it now.

Her orgasm, the spa and the massage at last relaxed her into sleep. Her final thoughts were of the roses he'd sent. Had she ever thought it was over, really over? After him where would she go in life? What could ever come close to what she'd found in him? What use would she ever be to another man when all the time she would be looking for someone to equal him? In his words he still loved her. She was so in love with him that the intensity of her emotional and sexual response to him drowned out the quieter voice of pure love. How easily he proclaimed this independent state of love with him as king and her as queen. She was a humble citizen in the swarming republic of love, singing the songs of the revolution that Randolph had brought to her life. Once the mob went home and the banners were put away, she would see what stood and what had fallen. She would know if it was a place where she could live.

Chapter 25

She had no idea of the time. The jet lag, the place lag, the conflicts and confusions about her life and her job had left her with a sense of blankness. She was so many contradictions that she seemed canceled out and left without any center. A maid brought her strong coffee and operated the polarized glass to reveal the panorama of New York City under a blue sky. OK, she could see where she was. So far, so good.

She threw on a luxury bathrobe and went to a desk where there was a computer terminal. She remembered that Shannon had advised her to check her Sackman-Platinum account. She tapped in the codes and then sat motionless staring at the screen. Her one million eight hundred thousand dollars had grown to nine million two hundred thousand. A large red envelope icon was flashing at the corner of the screen. She brought up the message.

"I was aiming for ten but thoughts of you distracted me. Your fault not mine. Ti amo xxxx."

This was crazy and getting crazier. Money like this wasn't real, it was no more than numbers on a sheet of paper. Someone was knocking at the door, she had to focus on actual real life. She shut down the screen and opened the door to Shannon.

"Hey, did you check your account?" she asked, breezing in with a huge smile.

"I did, how, what?"

"He played our accounts as well. The guy's a genius."

"Did you make some cash?"

"Sure, I won't embarrass him by telling you how much in case he made less for you."

Kaitlyn drew a deep breath and held it. A huge impertinent question was bursting to escape. Shannon was a senior Scotland Yard detective. She was married to an aristocrat with a mansion but wealth like this felt dirty, improper.

"Shannon, should we be involved with these guys like this? Okay, Randolph's got some trading method that scoops the markets but is it moral for us to profit from it? We're cops for Christ's sake."

"I'm a regular citizen who chose a good bank."

Kaitlyn sighed. She'd been brought up to believe in hard work and honesty. Her self-image and vision had been small and gray perhaps. Shannon reached out a hand to take hers.

"You're honest and good. The cops need that. Look, we've got a meeting at 11:30. The maid will help you dress. Just bide your time, relax and wait until we've met Stella Boursellino. Then we'll really talk okay?"

She nodded her agreement. She'd met Stella and had liked her even though she was confused by the lie about her riding accident. Did any of these guys ever just fly straight and level?

She showered, ate a fabulous feast of fresh fruit and assessed her dress for the day. Platinum, fucking platinum, she was just so fucking sick of platinum. The suit hung on a rail that the maid wheeled in. The Versace silk-wool suit was gorgeous with flared pants. The fit was perfect. She'd become a corporate executive. There was also a platinum pendant and platinum earrings in the form of the vulture and bank roll logo. What the hell? She was going to do it and go with the flow. At least they'd allowed her scarlet Prada five-inch heels. She took a twirl in the mirror. To be honest, and honesty was her endless curse, she looked fabulous.

Finally Emmanuelle came back and waxed her legs, fixed her nails and makeup, and blow-dried her hair. Some minutes she could live like this forever. Some minutes she wanted to run away screaming. She laughed to herself. At least she'd be well dressed.

She joined Shannon in the lobby. She was wearing a deep blue pinstripe business suit with skirt and low heels.

"God, you look stunning, Kaitlyn."

"You too. I thought you might be in platinum."

"There's a hierarchy here. You're operational level."

There was that *operator* word again. She decided to let it rest for now. It was odd that Shannon was dressed down, wore little makeup and no jewellery. She was a beautiful woman and her police superior, but today she was trying not to shine. So many, many questions crowded in her mind.

"Let's go see the boss, I guess," she said.

160

The Lincoln town car sped them through the Holland Tunnel. Inwardly she shuddered at the claustrophobic eeriness of the reflected car lights on the cold tiles. It was a relief to burst out into the sunlight and cruise up to the grand entrance of Platinum Trading Center. A posse of assistants swarmed around the car. Her platinum suit seemed to have excited some frenzy of attention as if she were the queen bee moving between egg chambers. Several attendants joined them in the elevator and rode up and up into the sky. Kaitlyn avoided eye contact. They must have mistaken her for someone else. Shannon wore a fixed faint smile like the Mona Lisa. They stopped and the door opened into a huge room with a 360-degree glass panorama. The predominant tone was, as always, platinum. Gold and crystal chandeliers provided some relief as did the flooring of exquisite white Carrara marble. Persian carpets broke up the vista along with several statues of Greek gods in gold and naturally an enormous corporate vulture with bankroll. In the center of the room was an executive desk larger than a king-size bed. Around it was a semicircle of seating formed by a continuous buttoned white leather sofa.

"Welcome to headquarters," said Stella Boursellino from her wheelchair. Kaitlyn extended her hand to shake.

"Come on, we're international. It's polite to kiss."

Kaitlyn kissed her cheeks as did Shannon. Behind her stood André with whom she had worked *and killed* in Paris. He too was dressed in platinum.

"Come in to my office," said Stella with a flourish of her arm.

She spun the chair and whizzed ahead of them to her desk, beckoning them to take seats on the white leather. She ordered coffee from a liveried butler and beamed a warm smile.

"Kaitlyn, in a few minutes we can talk. I hope you've been cared for?"

"Sure, I've had everything. I'm overwhelmed by everything. I don't know what to say."

Stella nodded.

"You've had to go through a lot and we would never have wanted it in that way. You've done so, so well. I just can't tell you how impressed we are."

"We?"

"Wait, once we have coffee we'll talk."

Some staff served a dark brew like she'd never tasted. She felt the hit of the caffeine in her brain.

"OK, please secure the office, guys. Jeff, Michael, come on in please."

Everybody left the room. Two dark-suited middle-aged men appeared from a spiral staircase which led to a mezzanine floor and took places on the crescent sofa. A green lamp lit up on Stella's desk. She continued.

"Ladies and gentlemen, the room is now secured. No one can leave or come in. First let me welcome Detective Inspector Shannon Knightsmith of Scotland Yard London, Countess of Bloxington and wife of our good friend and client Spencer Chamberlain-Knightsmith, Earl of Bloxington. This is Shannon's first time at a meeting on this level. We knew her before and had to bring her fully inside when Randolph got himself arrested."

The two men and Shannon laughed. Stella allowed herself a smile.

"You see the trouble you caused Kaitlyn. Now the poor girl has no idea what I'm talking about and in her position I'd be yelling and calling the cops. But Kaitlyn is not me and she's a very special operator. By the way you're a show-stopper to look at."

All the others mumbled agreement.

"Stella—am I some form of exhibit or what?"

She was sick of this mystery.

"No, but you're a rare specimen. Let me pose you a question and I want a frank answer. What do you make of Sackman-Platinum Bank?"

"You seem to control the world. You have infinite wealth, no morals or care for mankind. A lot of your presentation is crude, greedy, and brash. You appeal to the worst aspects of mankind and a good number of your clients are the lowest scum on the planet. You're boastful and in-your-face with all your conspicuous consumption. The whole image is a vile boast and seems to take delight in trampling the small guy and pushing your toys like planes and ships down the throats of the poor. Death is a business tactic and human life counts for nothing against the pursuit of money. I could go on but there, that's my take on it so far. Oh, by the way, you guys have

162

made me rich on paper. I regard that as a stinking bribe and I don't want it."

Stella leaned back and held out her arms. The two guys in suits applauded. Shannon looked at her with a half grin.

"That's just so wonderful, Kaitlyn. Randolph saw you right from the start. I was dubious, but as usual, he was right. Okay, let me introduce the suits. First we have Jeff; he's Director of the C.I.A. Second we have Michael; he's head of the W.I.F."

"What's that?" asked Kaitlyn as her brain screamed quietly inside her head.

"W.I.F. is the World Intelligence Forum. It's a conglomeration of folks like your British MI5, MI6, the FBI, the CIA and agencies from all around the globe. Let me tell you the most important fact. Sackman-Platinum is a front; a *front*. It's the biggest and most powerful crime fighting agency ever conceived. It is such a good front that it is also the world's richest company. If you want to look like the real deal, *be the real deal*."

Kaitlyn studied the serious-looking men: they had to be two of the most important people in the world.

"Let me carry on but please stop me with any questions. Once the Internet became so powerful the forces of law and order tried to respond. Half the traffic in cyberspace relates to crime, terrorism, and downright evil. Crime has never been so organized. The crooks can know everything about anyone and few people aren't open to blackmail. Local, national, and international agencies tried to step up. Guys like the FBI, MI5, the CIA and all those organizations are like household brands of soap. They work in the public eye. Basically, they're no more than simple cops hoping to catch a burglar by walking the beat. Drugs, human trafficking, organized fraud by corrupt regimes, have grown in the warm sun of cyberspace. The good guys knew they were losing the battle. Jeff saw the problem clearly but the US government and all the others of the civilized world didn't want to face up to the problem. Can you imagine a president or a prime minister going to his people to say, 'Our agencies have lost the battle to control crime. We need to ask you for a ten percent increase in taxes even to have a chance of staying where we are.'?"

Something of what she was saying was working its way into Kaitlyn's mind.

"I've killed a couple of guys on your behalf. They seemed like crooks but no trial, no lawyers. How can that be right?"

"You acted completely in self-defense. Our organization is covered by something called the Washington Accord. When crime started to run the planet, the president of the USA and the heads of all civilized governments signed a general dispensation for all law and order operatives working with the consent of the WIF. You killed, but it was lawful and you need think no more about it. None of those presidents know the truth about Sackman-Platinum."

"So who does know?"

"This is it, except for Randolph Quinn, and he's still in Italy finishing a mission."

"That's only seven people."

"Yeah and to be honest that's six too many."

"Christ. Why me?"

"Randolph happened to come across you. I believe you chased a couple of armed thugs and then karate chopped some Mafia barbarian in the throat for dessert. He's a sucker for that sort of girl."

Shannon chuckled. The comedy spread to the two men and finally to Kaitlyn herself.

"I was having an angry day. So Stella, please tell me how it works."

"Did you see our other building? It's brash and trash. It's shallow and vile and bangs out the message of heartless greed. Crooks flock to us and we launder their money. Do you realize that at least forty percent of the world economic activity is crime related? We handle nearly all of that cash. Also we know what every crook is into. Sometimes we inform on one load of crooks to another group. It's great to watch crocodiles eating crocodiles. We steadily supply information on our clients to the forces of law and order and believe me it's beginning to show. None of these agencies know the source of the tipoff and never will. We are entitled to act with lethal force to prevent us being uncovered."

"And you're the richest people on Earth."

"We have to be because we have to be the real deal. We can't look like anything other than cold-hearted greed-monsters. We employ fifty-eight thousand people and all on good wages. All the same when we closed the account of that

164

Valmir Rudovic we retained his twenty-nine billion dollar deposit. Randolph will find a home for that."

"I'm stunned, to be honest. You still haven't told me why I've been recruited."

"Let me ask you a question. What do you make of Randolph?"

"He's some sort of techie geek genius with looks of a God and unshakable belief in himself. He's also fearless."

"And he fell for you. You locked him up but you took him a cup of tea when you didn't have to bother. He saw your humanity, honesty, and courage. He grew up in a hard place without a lot of love. Randolph is the driving power and brain behind this business. He gets what he wants and he wanted you to keep."

Michael the director of the World Intelligence Forum spoke up.

"He invented the Accelerated Laser Trading method. He saw at once he could scoop the riches of the world. He'd grown up around crooks, his own father was stabbed by protection-racket thugs. Instead of selling out for money he took his invention to your government and they arranged for his meeting with the CIA. Americans act while the Brits form a committee. That was the beginning of Sackman-Platinum, the richest business the world has ever seen. Drug importation is down by fifteen percent, child prostitution has been wiped out of many areas of the world. I believe the Albanian Mafia have been seriously weakened."

"So he wasn't selling stuff from a suitcase when you gave him a job, Stella?"

"Well, he had a prototype laser in a suitcase. He gave *me* a job. I was already well known as a Wall Street investor so I looked the part."

So now she knew. What could she think or make of it all? Suddenly she was part of one of the most exclusive groups in the world. She was at the pinnacle of law enforcement, but she would never be able to tell the truth about her life. No wonder Shannon had said she could never go back. There was only one place she wanted to be."

"I want to see Randolph," she said.

"Of course we'll fix that. These bloody Albanian mafiosi are some sort of dinosaur throwback to the old days. Did you know they'd turned up here with machine guns to withdraw their money?"

"I can imagine. Why not just pay them off?"

"One of our regular office girls was shot, but luckily she was OK. Randolph is a fiercely loyal man and he swore to her he would personally close their account. Things got out of hand as I'm sure you noticed. They were better organized and stronger than he thought. We deal with the sort of people who just have to know not to cross us. At the moment he's got a small bit of business to finish in Italy. Trust me, this is the end of his James Bond career."

"I want to go to him now, whatever he's doing. You were happy for me to die when I didn't know what was going on, so you can't object to me risking my life when I do know."

Stella nodded seriously.

"You've proved everything you can. You know how vital it is to keep the truth among us. We would not tolerate exposure."

"I understand that."

"And thanks again for helping to save my life in Paris. We'll have a plane at JFK tonight. You'll be flying to Fiumicino airport in Rome. Don't miss the Vatican if you get the chance."

Chapter 26

A deep happiness was bursting inside her. She was going to be with him again and that was all that mattered in the world. He wasn't a crook, she wasn't going to jail. They had a chance, even though she had no idea where it would all go between them. According to Stella, he had one more job in Rome and that would be the end of the violence and the killing. At least she would be at his side. Just one more moment of madness and then a real life could begin. Surely he couldn't fall at this final hurdle. Surely he didn't want to kill and keep killing? She could never truly love such a man despite her longing for him with every cell of her body.

They ate a fabulous lunch in the executive restaurant. Beluga caviar, quail eggs, and truffles had been just words to her. Here they were everyday items. André took them on a tour of the trading floor and explained the bank's day-to-day operations. The Accelerated Laser Trading system was connected directly to Wall Street. Offices in every capital city with financial markets were connected to the dealing centers. Hundreds of traders scooped profits from every transaction.

"If these guys don't grab a five-million-dollar bonus every year, they're out of here," he explained calmly. "Most ordinary trading is done by robot computers. Shares, bonds, and gold are traded automatically as the market fluctuates. A unit of anything can be bought and sold several times a second and we harvest a commission on every trade. Our record in this building alone is seven billion dollars in eighteen minutes and all done by tireless machines."

The dedication to greed fascinated her. Every second of every day in every point of the world the operation grasped and competed for money. They would never stop until they had consumed and controlled everything. The robots scanned and spied on every money movement and swept the take into Sackman-Platinum's grasp. Their 24-hour TV News channels created mood swings and enhanced the surge of the markets like an octopus sweeping prey into its mouth. She thought of the life she'd known as an ant on the forest floor, struggling to pay her rent and car finance. Did these guys ever look down?

"Does the bank ever think of poorer people or the problems of this world?" she asked.

André sighed.

"Look, we're Sackman-Platinum. We're about wealth. Some of these Silicon Valley guys like to big themselves up with showing off their love of mankind. That's what they get off on. They get their big teeth in the magazines by giving a million to some suffering people or something like that. Work with us and we'll get you wealth. We don't market social conscience. That's what we do and that's what our clients like."

He finished with a wink. Of course he knew the whole story but the day-to-day reality was nonetheless disturbing.

At last they were free to breathe the air of regular life. She turned to Shannon as the Lincoln dropped them back at Platinum Tower. It was the first time they'd been able to talk since the meeting.

"I'm just so overwhelmed by everything I've heard. Did it come as a shock to you?"

"It sure did. Stella had phoned my husband and asked if I could get Randolph out of jail. I knew her because my husband is a big client of the bank. I contacted Stella and she flew in from Paris to tell me the whole deal. I bamboozled everyone with the witness protection story and then had to set it up as if it were for real. It was then I realized that someone inside the Force was tipping off the bad guys. I couldn't tell you the story or what I knew because we just didn't know you. I had to make all sorts of pretenses and tell you outright lies. I couldn't risk you learning the truth about the bank. Randolph wanted you and I was pleased to have a straightforward cop on the inside."

"Even if I could have wound up dead?"

"Yes, you're a cop. You could wind up dead on any street corner if some crazy terrorist drives a car at you."

Kaitlyn nodded. Shannon was right of course.

"Randolph didn't need to start a war with these thugs."

"He didn't need to but they came for him and hurt that office girl. These people, these murderers, torturers, rapists have gotten used to swaggering about in this world. Law enforcement shied away from conflict. Sometimes, Kaitlyn, you have to fight fire with fire. I'll be honest with you. If Sackman-Platinum clear the world of this vermin, I don't care how they do it. If they stop terrorists getting hold of machine guns, I don't care either. If no kid gets conned and put into prostitution I'm voting for that. It's not politically correct or moral, but that's what I feel."

Kaitlyn's own thoughts were conflicted. Shannon was a top Scotland Yard detective. She'd been there and she'd done it for many more years than her. This was not the place or time to debate the rights or wrongs. Every time she relaxed, thoughts of Randolph filled her.

"I guess I should be thinking about my job. I mean I can't just walk away."

"As of now you're free. I'll get you signed off on sabbatical leave. If you want to pick up your career in the Metropolitan Police it will always be there in some sort of role. For now you're an employee of the bank. Whatever you do next in Rome is down to you. Potentially you have a fabulous life ahead of you. My advice is not to get killed or maimed just when it's looking so good."

"I can't argue with that advice. Thanks, Shannon."

Kaitlyn hugged her warmly, sensing an edge of sadness or regret in the other woman's body language.

"This has all been about me. Where's your life going now?"

"Back to work, but being inside the Sackman-Platinum loop may mean some changes. I could stop, be a lady of the manor or just tour around the world. I'm a bit pissed that I'll never be able to tell my husband the truth about the bank. We've been trying for a baby but it's not happening. He was married before and he has a son, so at least it looks like he's got the goods. He wants a baby with me so much but I've got a while before I need to start panicking."

Suddenly she realized this top-cop super woman had a real human life with doubts and fears.

Kaitlyn rolled up her sleeve to reveal her tattoo.

"I'll put Ishtar on the job. She's the female goddess of bloody near everything including fertility." She took Shannon's hand and placed it on her arm. "The power is flowing in to you. All you have to do is keep your mind open."

Shannon smiled.

"I should say that it's pagan superstition."

"Keep your mind open and don't dismiss it. If it's rubbish, it's rubbish. Now the spirit of the goddess can be inside you if you want it."

"OK, I've got it. Spencer is flying out tonight and we'll spend a couple of days in New York. He needs a break. Maybe we'll try things out with some Ishtar power."

They embraced again and took the elevator to their penthouse suites. She had a while before she needed to go to the airport. She was disoriented by the time difference and by all that she'd seen and learned. She checked her bank balance. The daily interest on her deposit had already pushed her total to over ten million dollars. What could she think, should she think? She noticed an expensive looking black box covered in velvet on the bedside cabinet. The vulture and bank roll badge was inlaid. She opened it and gasped. It was a solid platinum vibrator set with sapphires and diamonds. A plaque inside the lid read. *"With the compliments of Sackman-Platinum. Feel the buzz of wealth."*

She stared at it. Who would have put it there? Perhaps this was the normal corporate executive gift. She put her hand to her mouth. It was gross, gorgeous, decadent. Tempting. She ran her fingers up and down. The gems were flush with the metal so that it was completely smooth. Out of curiosity she turned the jewel encrusted crown at one end and the machine purred a range of rhythms. She was alone, thinking of her man, she had a while to relax. No, she couldn't. What sort of woman was she?

For a second she held it to her groin. She couldn't, she just couldn't. She walked to the window control-panel and de-polarised the glass. The vista of New York was spread before her. She pushed a leather office relining chair right up to the glass, the toy still in her hand. She sat down as if on the edge of time and space. Maybe it wouldn't hurt to check it out, just once. She opened the fastener of her pants and spread her legs so that her sex gazed out above the city. She let the tireless buzz of wealth run across her panties to her groove. She loved it. She was such a greedy girl. Oh God, she absolutely fucking loved it.

At last she had satiated her physical yearning for that bastard, Randolph Quinn, and was indulging her relaxed body in the spa, when Emmanuelle came in. She massaged her, fixed her hair, nails, and makeup. She selected a blue Michael Kors leopard skin stretch-knit dress and pink Gucci Queen Margaret leather pumps.

"I'll hope to see you again, madam," said Emmanuelle.

"For sure I'll ask for you whenever I come to New York."

The girl smiled and held her eyes.

"You're my most beautiful ever client."

"I'm not sure I'll ever get used to being served."

"You are a pleasure, madam. It doesn't feel like work."

How wonderful it was to be desired and told that you're beautiful. How deep did wealth sink into the soul? She'd always wondered about all those failed bankers diving from the top of the building, rather than face up to poverty. She was beginning to see how it would feel. Now she had just one mission. She could sleep a little on the plane and arrive refreshed in Rome. Then she'd be sexed up and ready to greet her man.

The Lincoln town car swept through the security barrier and rolled up to the steps of the aircraft. How she loved this ease and luxury. How she was still ashamed of her decadent acceptance of wealth. She'd expected it to be the same one that had brought her from London. A quick glance told her that it was a 747 like the one Randolph had been using. She smiled inwardly at her memories of the upper deck. Just how many planes did this business have? A cabin crew guy was opening the car door. She stared at him as he smiled.

"Randolph!"

He took her into his arms, a borrowed crew hat crooked on his head.

"I couldn't do much without you in Rome so I figured I'd just take a ride over to keep you company."

She clung to him, feeling the thrill of his hard muscle and the warmth of his deep brown eyes. There was so much to say, so much to ask but her joy at being with him pushed all else aside.

"I don't suppose you want to know I still love you," he said.

"Keep telling me, I'll let you know."

He kissed her lips with a passion that was still soft and tender. She let her breasts thrill to the closeness of his male strength just under his clothing. A delicious tension tweaked her groin. She could feel his arousal against her as she tightened herself to rebuild her need. She would never have masturbated if she'd known he was going to show up on the plane.

"We have immediate priority runway clearance for the next ten minutes. Shall we talk privately upstairs?"

He followed her up the steps, his hand gentle but firm in the small of her back. They strapped in for takeoff and watched New York slip away into the night as the plane headed out across the Atlantic Ocean.

She knew she'd been drinking too much but still couldn't resist the Veuve La Salle champagne that he poured.

"The guys who make this are good clients," he said.

He looked so handsome, so confident in his Armani business suit. He talked like a successful business man. And yet he still had a mission, could still end with his brains splattered on a sidewalk. Secretly she was pleased she'd reduced her tension with Mr Platinum. It meant she could talk turkey without too much interference from her sexual desire for him.

"Stella tells me you've got a final mission before this horrible business is over."

His face was serious.

"I can't deny that. If you spend all day painting your house, the job's not done until you've washed your brushes and put away your ladder. I've just got to tidy up."

She wanted to yell and scream at him. He was alive, rich, young, and in her lust she would offer herself to him on almost any terms. Why the hell did he need to risk it all for the sake of some dumb thug?

"If you really loved me like you say, you'd care about my feelings."

"I do care and you're worrying about nothing. I do want you to learn to trust me, Kaitlyn. We had our little disagreement before on this matter and you know that I'm very nearly always completely right."

"You're a cheeky bastard, Quinn. When did you ever admit to being wrong?"

"Just this minute, because I thought you'd be in bed with me by now."

She tried not to choke on her champagne.

"You are ... I don't even know a word for you."

"Trustworthy, sexy, needy."

"I give up."

"Just focus on the needy. I need you."

"In bed, at 38,000 feet?"

"Girls tell me height doesn't matter."

"What girls and when did they tell you?"

"When I was a weedy brat in the school yard. I was a late developer."

How could she not be in love with him? He'd re-found his old cheeky arrogance and for sure not lost his looks. She gave up.

They climbed the stairs. He stripped naked and lay on the bed.

"I didn't want you to feel coy or vulnerable. Let's see if you excite me at all."

He relaxed back and watched her undress. She couldn't help letting her eyes focus on his cock. She let go her bra and ran her hands over her breasts. His hands were behind his head as his erection pumped his shaft upwards. She slipped off the dress but kept her panties in position. Now he was rock hard and straining. She slipped her hand inside her panties and sucked the thumb of her free hand, like she'd seen pole dancers do.

"You're a natural show girl," he growled in his deep voice.

"Didn't I tell you about my double life as a Soho stripper?"

"Now's your moment."

"I was busking topless in the snow with my piano accordion on a corner in Greek Street. A greasy slicked-back guy in alligator shoes with a beer gut, black shirt, and white tie told me he'd put me in the movies, but I'd have to show him my talent."

"With or without your squeezebox?"

"That's a very personal question for a girl."

173

"I love you so much."

His tone had changed. He really did love her or at least believed he did. To hell with it, why hold back?

"I love you too."

He sprang from the bed and pulled her to him, not kissing, not touching but simply connecting. This was her moment to hit below the belt.

"I won't believe any of your words of love if you are going to risk all our future with some stupid violence in Rome."

"My job in Rome has nothing to do with my feelings for you."

"Exactly, you think I can make love with you and then prop up your head as you choke on your own blood?"

"Hey, that guy did get you into the movies. I've seen that story."

"You're a jerk."

"You keep saying that. Let's say hello to each other properly."

In an effortless sweep, he carried her to the bed. He laid her down and propped himself on an elbow to look at her.

"You're so beautiful. When I first saw you I wondered how the hell I could meet someone like you working as a traffic cop."

"Heaven made it possible by turning a spare angel into a traffic cop."

"That doesn't explain the beauty."

"I'd forgotten to take my ugly pills. Multi-billionaires kept sticking to me every time I left heaven."

He laughed and kissed his way down to her breast. His tongue licked her nipple, his lips drew her in while his other hand gently teased the other side. Twin pings of arousal tingled in her sex. He kissed her lips deeply, warmly, lovingly, as his hand slipped to the hood of her clitoris. Oh God, she thought she'd calmed her lust. His presence made her want to come, let him control her, let him know her more than she knew herself. She reached for his cock as he eased her up the slope to her oblivion. He'd linked to her brainwaves, her sounds, her need, her tension. The pulsing demand of his cock matched the grip of her own desire in her clitoris. She felt the wetness of his tip matching the wetness of her groove. She could sense his musk as she built and climbed and climbed.

His voice was deep and groaning as she held him. She was losing control, couldn't hold on. This was her point, teasing, hiding, teasing. His cock pulsed again in her hand as he sensed her moment. His response to her thrilled her as he quickened her last steps and then pressed and soothed the delicious burst of her orgasm, spreading the convulsions of helpless pleasure into her belly, her thighs, her bloody soul. She let out a groan, bestial, shameless, and rooted somewhere in the flower-perfumed sweat of the jungle life force. She was weak and open, wanted his hot cock pulsing his cum into her belly. She was a void. She was the sucking heat of the female, the juice and blood of existence in all its tyrannies of life and lust. She wanted his hard ruthless push inside her, needed to offer that peculiar power of her weakness to that male passion to possess. She pulled his cock to her entrance.

"Fuck, do it."

He was hot, thick and filling, pushing up to her roof. She cried out as he plunged to his limit, withdrew in an aching tease and then drove in again, opening her, spreading her, holding her hard, while he shared his unstoppable pleasure with her. He was hitting her spot, each time jolting her further up that slope, pushing her up further and further, further and further. She could feel the pressure of his tension, ripe and riper, longing to burst. She could smell wild male sex musk, something she had caught in the air when he was close to release. Something she craved. Her mind flashed back to his cock in his own hand, pulsing out his hot cum onto her belly because he couldn't contain his desire for her. No shame, no mind, no restraint. She dropped her hand to her clitoris to bring herself exactly to his moment of release. He shuddered and convulsed with pleasure as his cum spilled and spilled into her pussy. Her fingers clawed the last inch of her climb as she let go, her belly pulsing to the same rhythm as his seed jetting from his cock helpless in abandon to her.

"Why the fuck am I thinking of babies?"

"Because you're never going to have one with anyone but me," he growled, kissing her lips.

"You're an arrogant bastard."

"I know you can't help it, but you keep saying that."

Chapter 27

The plane taxied to a far corner of Rome Airport. It was 2 p.m. European time.

"We've no business today. I have arranged an exclusive tour of the Vatican later," he said.

"Just like that?"

"Why not?"

"How do you fix up that kind of thing?"

"You call a guy at the Vatican Bank and they come up with a cardinal. We do a lot of business with these gentlemen."

"Dear Lord, don't tell me that God is a Mafia front?"

"If you leave God and the pope out of the picture, the Vatican Bank does have a colorful profile. Sackman-Platinum is in there big time these days. The cardinals were a bit naive and now and again some hoods have taken advantage."

"I've just got a horrible feeling that our *business* in Rome is going to involve the church."

"No chance. We've got two executives on the board and they keep everything tidy. We've just got one meeting in the morning and the only angel there will be you."

"You're a cheesy jerk."

"But you are an angel, you told me."

The Alfa Romeo took the freeway into Rome, another place she had never been. The Vatican looked like a huge fortress surrounded by miles of uncountable bricks in a continuous wall. The car sped into an open courtyard. Beyond was the great dome of St Peter's. A priest in purple robes met them and shook hands.

"Randolph, so good to see you again."

"Kaitlyn, this is Patrick."

She shook hands and followed the circuit along galleries of impossibly beautiful paintings, statues, and tapestries. They gazed up at Michelangelo's ceiling of the Sistine Chapel. She felt small, humble, and insignificant in the atmosphere of such a place. So many of the images were reproduced in every form of world media. If there was a center to her civilization, to her belief in the law, right and wrong, then this was the place, with or without faith. Finally they moved on to Saint Peter's Basilica, its very enormity offering itself as a certainty, a Bible in stone that proclaimed to her as much the hand of the craftsman, the engineer, the laborer as it did the hand of God.

"I want to light a candle," she said.

"Sure, you surprise me. What's it for?" asked Randolph.

"For a friend with a bit of a problem, that's all."

Patrick led them to a small side chapel. She had no idea of which saint was in charge of which department of human affairs and she didn't want to show her ignorance. She didn't even know if she had any religious faith. She lit a candle and stood back to watch it in the dusky light of the basilica. She couldn't say it was a prayer but it was a plea beyond herself. The flame embodied the idea of life perhaps, the life consuming the form of that simple candle. Nature was exchanging the lifeless body of the wax and string into a living thing, a warming thing, a dangerous thing, a light that would live for a span of time as would all mortal life forms. This fragile flame was a living presence in this great building of stone, like all creatures living their tiny span of time in the pitiless universe. She smiled at her own muddled philosophy. After all, she'd already put the pagan goddess Ishtar on the job.

"Let's take a walk to the Trevi Fountain. I love to soak up the atmosphere of Rome," said Randolph.

They walked the narrow cobbled back streets, past the Pantheon to the fountain. They were tourists, lovers hand in hand. She could spoil this time with questions about tomorrow, but tomorrow would come and it would make no difference whatever she said. They both threw the cliché of coins into the fountain.

"We've got a table at Il Convivio. It's close to my little apartment," he said.

"Of course you have a place in Rome."

"Sure, but I don't mind sharing."

"Where is your actual home?"

"Now that is a good question. I was going to ask you where you thought it should be."

His answer was flippant in the same way that so many of his responses were evasive. She'd been thinking back to the comments from the meeting in New York. The serious guy had said that Randolph hadn't had much love and that his father had been stabbed. Was that a place she should go?"

"Where was home when you were a kid?"

"I told you, New Addington Estate in South London."

"What was it like?"

"Shit."

"And your father was stabbed?"

He stopped abruptly and stared at her.

"Who told you that? I don't do all that stuff. I was Lee Smith then. That world is closed down."

"I'd like to know you, I mean really know you."

"No, you wouldn't."

"The love word slips so easily from your lips into my panties. If you knew anything about love you'd understand that I want to know you."

"That's a low blow, girl."

"It's true, that's what love involves."

He smiled and nodded.

"I get it. You do love me and that's why you want to know."

"I walked into that didn't I? Just tell me a bit about yourself as a kid."

"All right. We were always broke and my father was a drinker and a bit of a wife beater. My mother left me with him and ran away. Then he hit me and moved in some old cow who drank more than him. Then they hit each other. He worked on and off for a guy who ran sex chat phone lines with a couple of old, worn out prostitutes. Some thugs came round for their protection racket payment. His boss couldn't or wouldn't pay so they stabbed him and my dad did his one noble act of a lifetime and tried to help him. He bled out on the floor. No one saw or knew anything of course and the police couldn't get any evidence. Familiar story?"

"What happened to you?"

"They put me in a kids' home, but I soon got out. Then one day I met you and my life began."

"That's a terrible story."

"You're not that bad."

"Randolph, you don't always have to bury your feelings with tricky answers."

"Don't I? It's always worked for me. What did they tell you on your psychology degree course?"

"They told me that human beings are more complex than they can even imagine themselves."

"Look, the Queen of England always says don't complain, don't explain. If it's good enough for Her Majesty then it's good enough for me. Now she really is rich."

"You genuinely don't want to talk about it?"

"I just did. I bet you're worried now that I'm going to get drunk and beat you up. Apples don't fall far from the tree and genes is genes."

"So you fear that?"

He sighed and pulled her into his arms.

"Maybe. Maybe yes, in the back of my mind I suppose I always think it must be in me. Maybe I've been too quick to use the love word. I can see that and I can see that would frighten a woman if she thought it was all too fast, so I'm sorry about that."

"Randolph, please I didn't mean that. You're full of yourself but you're easily hurt."

"Who's going to start crying first, me or you?"

"I don't want any crying, but I'd never care if you felt that way."

"I know. Look, I can't believe I love you. It's not a feeling I know too well. I'm a banker for Christ's sake. How can I be a technical and financial genius and also possess emotional intelligence?"

"Thank God you're not a boxer because you'd always get off the ropes wouldn't you?"

"I'd keep still for you."

"You're a jerk."

"I'm not even going to say anything."

"I know, I do keep saying that."

They arrived at the restaurant in Vicolo dei Soldati, a tiny cobbled side street. She dismissed her cares about the morning even though she was aching to know what was going to happen. This evening was a time to get inside him and there may never be another.

He ordered the taster menu of a selection of wonderful Italian food with a range of wines. The staff greeted him like an old friend. She could see his happiness at somehow being part of a family. He was the richest man in the world but in truth he had little interest in money. He'd been happy to stroll the streets like any other man.

"What drives you, Randolph?"

"Fear of being broke, and if you've ever had no food in the cupboard and no cash, that fear never goes away."

"I don't think you'll ever be broke."

"No one thought that the banking system would collapse in 2007."

She took a deep breath. He wasn't quite ready to open up but she'd gotten on the inside.

"You didn't have to say sorry for the love word."

He turned his deep kind eyes to hers.

"I tend to bulldoze things you know. If I want something I go flat out."

"It's not a fault, it's lovely, it's the way you are and I love you right back in the same way."

"I don't want to open myself to your seductive psychological examination but the sensation's not as bad as I thought. No one has ever bothered to ask. You're so special, Kaitlyn. If you grow up, you know, not loved, then love is a hard thing to deal with. Can I appoint you as my consultant?"

"When do I start?"

"You've started."

"By the way, Randolph, thanks for the millions of dollars but I just can't accept all that. I'd rather have nothing and be with you as I was."

"That cannot be. You know the truth about Sackman-Platinum. We have to act the part and live the part. We've no choice in this."

She reached across the table and put her hand on his.

"Will we be alive to enjoy a meal like this tomorrow night?"

"Of course. This is a low key transaction tomorrow. We're going to go to see a guy and get him to see things my way. He's resisted me in the past but experience changes people. I'd like you to come with me, but I can do it alone. You've no idea how important trust is in this business. I asked you to trust me and you felt you couldn't. You went to New York and you came to understand a lot more. Now you're back with me and I'm asking you to trust me. It's not that I'm trying to test you...."

"But you're trying to test me all the same."

"Trust me, trust me, trust me."

Chapter 27

For the first time they lay together in bed without an urgency to make love. He kissed her face, her chin, the length of her nose. At her lips he took each one between his with the soft natural innocence of a leaf falling on moss. She was exhausted yet tense with her fears for the morning. If it all ended in spilled blood could she still want him? He wanted her to show him blind trust. It was an act of dominance as if he were God. She wanted a strong decisive man whom she could trust. She didn't have to go with him. There was no way she wasn't going to be at his side. Not long ago her life had been so simple and her thoughts so clear. Before Randolph Quinn.

His apartment was a short walk from the restaurant and surprisingly modest. It was a wonderful contrast to the brash corporate excess of his banker's life. It was an old building in La Via Giuseppe Zanardelli, a few steps from the River Tiber where the Umberto Bridge crossed to La Piazza dei Tribunali and the magnificent Supreme Court building. She awoke to the smell of strong fresh coffee and the chatter of Rai 24, the Italian rolling news channel. She pulled on a silk bath robe she'd found draped over an antique chair. He was in the kitchen, hair tousled, wearing nothing but Diesel jockey shorts. She slid her eyes around the tight curves of his butt and the bulge of his groin. This was serious male sculpture.

"You look gorgeous," he said.

"Thank you. I feel like I need that coffee."

A glance at the clock showed the time at 8:10 a.m. Her heart was pounding. This was it. This was the day. Whatever they were going to do, whatever the outcome she was just going to do it. She didn't want conflict about trust or morals. She'd decided to stick with him and that was that. Soon he would issue his instructions, issue her firearm, strap on his shoulder holster. Would she be stealing a truck? Would she be crashing a car into the freeway barriers?

"It's a wonderful sunny day out there," he said.

She nodded. She didn't care. She had no appetite but gulped down the coffee.

"I had your old suitcase recovered. This is a hoodie, jeans, and trainer day."

She didn't ask how he'd retrieved her case from the back of the car where they had left the dead body on the freeway in Milan. This was Sackman-Platinum and the world just raised the barriers and bowed. She showered, dressed, and sat on the edge of the bed. She felt a sudden surge of pleasure as she re-found her Ishtar jewellery that he had bought her in Harrods in London. All that seemed a lifetime away now. She put the ring on her finger. Maybe the goddess of combat would take her side. He seemed to sense her hair-trigger tension and stayed out of her comfort zone. He dressed in a Dolce & Gabbana leather motorcycle jacket and Versace jeans. He wore brown long-chiseled shoes and had left his facial stubble. He would look beautiful even on a morgue table. He handed her a motorcycle helmet. He was carrying a matching model and pushed a slim elegant briefcase inside his jacket.

"No guns?" she asked.

"Too difficult, with too many chances of collateral damage. We could end up killing a kid or something. I've seen your karate. This guy's a pushover. If he cuts up rough just chop his throat or kick his face in. I'll leave that to your own judgment. Trust me and let me do the talking."

She shrugged. She said she'd be at his side and that was all there was to say. She followed him down a flight of steps into a courtyard behind the building. He went to a door and wheeled out a cream colored Vespa scooter.

"You're not a Roman if you haven't got a scooter."

He started the motor and swung his leg over.

"All aboard," he called out.

They swept out into the traffic. His riding was moderate for Rome but outrageous by London traffic cop standards. If they survived the day, she'd offer him some road safety guidance. It was a truly gorgeous morning. How she would have thrilled to this ride in any other circumstances. They turned away from the river and headed into central Rome, once again swerving and beeping their way through the narrow cobbled streets around the Trevi Fountain. She could sense his impatient tension. At least they weren't carrying guns. At last they roared up to a building in a classy looking street. She caught the name Via Palestro. Randolph bounced the scooter up the curb and accelerated noisily through some tall iron gates and stopped under an elegant glass portico.

"This is it."

She stepped off while he calmly parked the bike and took off his helmet. She did the same and took a good long look at him.

"With a bit of luck we can deal with this in a few minutes and begin our lives. Always remember Kaitlyn that the job's not done until you've cleaned your tools and swept up the garbage."

She nodded. In previous missions she'd just been hijacked and had to respond without thought. This was in cold blood. She'd had half a day to think about it.

She had no words.

He pressed an intercom buzzer on the door. A male voice answered. Randolph responded in speed-of-light Italian. She took a deep breath.

The door clicked as an electric bolt drew back. He pushed his way in and strode through to a back room. Obviously he'd been here before and knew exactly where he was going. He was moving quickly, going straight in for the kill. She kept up, every sinew tight, all her reflexes wound to the limit.

He pushed open a heavy paneled door. A burly dark-haired guy was standing at a table at the back of a large room. It looked like he was making coffee in an elegant silver pot.

"Mario."

"Randolph—*che piacere vederti.*"

She braced herself. This must be some godfather scene where they kiss each other and the gorillas run in firing from the hip.

Both men were smiling with the warmth of the Italian sun in July. She glanced around the room to look for side doors or places to hide. There was a large office desk strewn with papers and some stuff looking like leaflets with African babies on the cover. There were posters on the wall of kids and school rooms. This was terrible. The guy must be a child trafficker or worse. Why the hell hadn't they brought guns? She'd started to read a poster when Randolph spoke.

"Kaitlyn, you're miles away. This is my great friend Mario, Dottore Mario Bartolo. He's the UNICEF guy here in Rome."

The guy stepped forward, warmly kissed both her cheeks and stood back as if to behold her like a painting.

"*Che bellezza*. You don't deserve this sort of class, Randolph. A girl like this needs an Italian husband, a man who knows beauty and style. You English never know how to show passionate love for a woman unless she gives you beer and chips."

"I love beer and chips," said Kaitlyn, finding herself oddly defensive of her man. What the hell was this? Apparently this was a bad guy?

"When are you going to stop slobbering over my fiancée and get us some coffee?"

"Fiancée, this is wonderful. Bambinis to come and big, big wedding. I bring everyone."

She stared open-mouthed at Randolph. He responded with a quick calming gesture with his hand. Mario was making coffee which smelled powerful. He was mid-thirties, smooth faced but with darkly shadowed cheeks like he shaved four times a day. He wore a stylish pale blue and cream striped blazer, a beige polo shirt and immaculately pressed dark pants. He gestured for them to sit down and returned to his desk with the cups of black ristretto.

"So, you come to bother me at my work, like I have nothing to do?"

"You love me really, Mario. You should never have left the bank. I'd have made you any title you wanted. You could have been Intergalactic Vice President."

"I'm happy. What else do I need in life?"

"You need about fifty billion dollars."

"Yeah and I need to be a beautiful film star or sing The Marriage of Figaro at La Scala for the pope."

"Can't fix that, but here's a check. I made it out to UNICEF."

"You're crazy. Any man can see you fall in love with a girl whose beauty stuns your brain."

"That's true as well. You want this or not?"

"I've told you before I can't accept your money. Everyone would want to know where the money came from and you won't admit to it. You want to be Mr Hardface, Mr Heartless, Mr Ruthless Bastard stamping on the children's toys. You want this image."

185

"This money could mean life and an end to suffering for a lot of kids. It can set up long-term structured programs. That means education, health, and the possibility of a decent life for millions. It's not from me. It's from the most beautiful girl in the world. If you want a face for a poster or for the magazines who want a story here she is."

She sat in stunned bewilderment. It wasn't hers. She'd thought they were coming here to beat up some criminal thug.

"Mario used to work for Sackman-Platinum. He traveled a lot and got a conscience. He loves kids or at least he keeps breeding them. I think he's stopped at six. He gave up wealth and riches to use his management and financial skills working for UNICEF. I've tried before to convince him to accept a donation."

"Yes and I tell you to let the world know that the cold-blooded bastard who runs Sackman-Platinum is really a nice guy. There's people out there who spit on your bank and on you for your greed and lack of mercy."

"Mario, it has to be that way."

"Yes, because you deal with animals who rip and eat each other and if you're not as strong they tear you to pieces too."

Randolph glanced at her. She understood why things had to be this way but Mario could never fully know. Now she understood why he'd been talking about some guy who wouldn't see things his way. She'd been looking around the office. This organization was the United Nations arm for children. Now she got it. This Randolph Quinn was a monster. He'd let her think that this final mission could be some horror of violence. Didn't he understand how she'd felt all night and on the way here?

"Excuse me, Mario, but Randolph, you're an utter bastard."

Mario clapped.

"Yes, ha—yes she see you like you are. She has such spirit. You will have to keep her busy so she is not always on your case. He hides himself this man. One night in Moscow we get the vodka and I learn of his home and childhood. He burns with anger this man. He knows what a childhood is and what it is *not* for many kids. I said no to his money because first I want that he show himself to the world."

"Randolph's right, Mario. This donation is from me. With the help of the bank I made a massive investment and made a

186

massive return. If I'm on Randolph's arm he can still be the same man of iron in business. People will see me and know that deep down I wouldn't love him if he were that bad."

"This is what you English call a compromise. You would make pasta with butter instead of olive oil if you needed to please a guy with a cow."

"What about the olive oil guys?" asked Randolph.

"You English would tell them you are developing special cows to eat olives and one day if they're patient they'll be millionaires."

"Mario should have gone into politics," he replied with a laugh.

"What I do with him eh?"

"Take the money, please," she said.

"For a beautiful angel of womankind, yes. For this heartless banker, no."

The two men hugged each other.

"Get that money paid in. You're losing interest every second."

"I'll be in touch with a breakdown of what we do with it."

"Ciao, Mario."

"I kiss your lovely bride one more time," he said performing noisy kisses on both her cheeks.

She couldn't believe he'd just handed over fifty billion dollars. They went back to the scooter.

"So you let me go through an ordeal of worry, you bastard. You don't want me to see your heart and that you care about kids."

"Who wants some rich jerk bigging himself up to get prizes and applause? In the Bible it says the wealthy already have their reward. You shouldn't reveal or brag about what you give to others, okay. Just for once, I didn't sin."

"For a ruthless monster you've got one hell of a heart."

"Don't forget the monster 'cause that sonofabitch is always here to protect us. Just the shadow or the reflection of him is all we need. Power is the biggest bluff. That's why the bullfighter wins and why love is always in the hands of the one who could walk away, like a mother who walks away from her child. I tell you now I'll never walk away from you."

Suddenly he'd surrendered. She was seeing the man inside she'd loved with some unwrapped instinct within herself since the moment they'd met.

"I'll never walk away from you, but you're still a bastard, Quinn."

"You do keep saying that and that's no way to speak to a fiancé."

"I see no ring. I'd never talk to a husband like that."

"I never dreamed you'd agree. I love you. I love you."

She re-buckled her helmet.

"Okay, fiancé?"

"Well, you're the ace traffic cop motorbiker. Show me how it's done. Take me to the Coliseum, then to the Colonna Traiana, then the Villa Medici and then anywhere you want. I'm going to sit here behind you and I'm going to love you ten percent more with every Roman column I see because the Romans did everything in tens."

"And when in Rome..."

FIN

A Message from Emma

Hello,

Thank you for reading '*WEALTH*' I hope you enjoyed it!

Please would you help me?

If you liked the book you've just read, I'd be forever grateful if you'd consider posting a short review. As an independent writer you guys really matter to me. It's very difficult for small authors to get visibility in the huge publishing machine, since we don't have the influence or advertising budgets of traditional publishers. Your review will give me a positive push and help other readers find a book they would enjoy.

Nothing long or complex is needed—just a sentence or two about what you enjoyed about the book.

Review Link: http://www.smarturl.it/WealthReview

Why not discover the stories all the other sassy female cops in the Passion Patrol? Check out the next section for links to other books in the Passion Patrol Series as well as a **free book** if you join my mailing list.

Many thanks for your interest in my stories.

Emma x

A Book For You You
FREE DOWNLOAD

Meet the Passion Patrol Team

Get this full-length suspense romance novel

FREE

when you line up with The Passion Patrol

...Join Emma Calin's VIP Reader Club

"Emma Calin has written another gripping romantic suspense with plenty of both."
P. Rees-Rohrbacker

If you enjoy my books, keep up to date with new releases, special offers and exclusive opportunities. As a valued reader, I'll send you a FREE e-book from my Passion Patrol Series – suspense romance novel GUILT. I email out a few newsletters each month with news snippets and background info to my stories, as well as sharing any bargains. Don't worry I will not bombard you! You may of course unsubscribe at any time.

Link: http://www.smarturl.it/LeadFromWealth Or scan the QR code:

Other titles by Emma Calin:
Passion Patrol Series Box Set 1

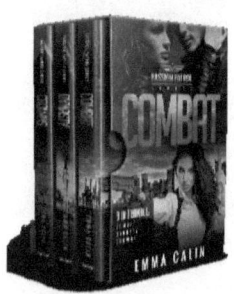

Grab the first three books in the *Passion Patrol Series* PLUS the companion cookbook to the second in the series in one **bargain** bundle. Titles included: *Combat, Dynasty, Seduction of Taste* and *Crowns*.

http://www.smarturl.it/webbox1

Or if you prefer to buy each ***Passion Patrol*** title individually…

Guilt, Combat, Crowns, Santa, Wealth, Power

Seduction of Taste

Seduction of Dynasty Plus (2-book bundle, Dynasty+Seduction of Taste)

Coming in 2019: ***Desire***

Combat

An early title in the *'Passion Patrol Series'*

Interpol cop, Anna Leyton, spirals down into a hopeless vortex of sexual and emotional passion as she fights to keep her professional cool. Who is deceiving whom in this fast-moving ride across continents? What motivates her art-loving prize bull of a lover, Freddie La Salle? The power of love and trust stands against greed and crime as conflicting forces grapple for that knockout punch.

A romance novel with a twist of suspense that will take you on a roller-coaster ride of passion, deception and love.

Link: http://www.smarturl.it/webcombat

Or scan QR code:

Dynasty

A sexy aristocrat. A wild-child inner city cop. A crime wave of passion.

http://www.smarturl.it/webdynasty

Blurb:

A steamy romance novel introducing a sassy female police officer who locks up criminals and always gets her man.

Moved out from the city after one-too-many maverick missions, Shannon discovers there's more going on in the sleepy country village than meets the eye. The son of a local aristocrat arouses suspicion of drug crime activity... but his widower father arouses more animal instincts!

Could she really mix with the British Royal Family? Can she risk her heart and career on yet another high-risk unauthorized investigation? Can she get justice for an innocent boy? Dare a kid from the gutter dream of being a countess?

Wild child inner city cop Shannon Aguerri walks a dangerous line between her methods and justice. When the bosses lose their nerve, she is transferred to green pastures to play out the role of a routine village cop. In Fleetworth-Green she encounters signs of people and drug trafficking and homes-in on serious millionaire criminals. As a loner she has attracted men but nothing has stuck. When she meets Spencer, the hunky and widowed Earl of Bloxington, there is an immediate rapport between them. Their social differences mean nothing to their passion and need. Already in the mix is an upper-class female rival who has long plotted her way into the earl's bed. The jealousy is an evil shade of green and the anger is a violent scarlet.

Often inhibited by a sense of duty and honor, Spencer is slow to reveal his feelings. When Shannon confronts him with the need to choose between her word and that of her rival, he does not immediately support her. All the same, when they are forced together to carry out a desperate rescue mission, their love is stronger than everything ranged against them.

Please note: This book contains joyful sex between adults in a consenting relationship. There is also strong language in high-stress police confrontations with criminals.

http://smarturl.it/webdynasty

Seduction of Taste

Hot Cops. Hot Crime. Hot Romance... Hot Food?

http://www.smarturl.it/CopsKitchen

Seduction of Taste is the companion cookbook to the hot romance novel Dynasty.

A total of thirty-one recipes from appetizers and main courses to suggestions for sandwich fillings at a traditional afternoon tea. Late night suppers and romantic meals for two.

With the cookbook you can tickle your taste buds as Emma Calin's full on total romance tickles your mind. If it touches the lovers' lips in the story, you can experience that moment with a meal cooked for your own special lover, be they a cool cucumber or a passionate pepper.

Read the romance, feel the passion, taste the love!

Or, grab the bumper gourmet edition—with both the story and recipe books combined and linked together though hyperlinks – ***Seduction of Dynasty Plus***.

Santa

For merciless people traffickers...

... Christmas doesn't exist.

Mature community cop Paula has a heart of gold, a heart broken by love. When gangsters force tough business man Max Muswell to hire exploited labour, Paula steps up to fight at his side.

Love forces up like snowdrops as the Christmas lamps turn on.

Poor and powerless workers face a cold and joyless future. Ruthless crooks fight back as Max and Paula face them down.

Can an unlikely Santa bring hope and joy?

Buy this book now to feel spirit of Christmas at any time of year.

http://www.smarturl.it/websanta

Guilt

Gunfire....

...A police dog is down.

Lonely dog handler Helen carries the guilt of survivor. Star singer and single father Marco is too guilty to sing. Both are too guilty to love.

They meet as an innocent animal fights for life. *Perhaps a hope is born?*

Terror fanatics close in on London, their target the Queen. A cop must follow her orders. A father must protect his child.

Love breaks laws and hearts.

Follow the lust and drama. Let go of the guilt. Enjoy the thrill of the action. Follow Marco and Helen to the climax of passion. Hold on for the ride to the triumph of love.

http://www.smarturl.it/webguilt

Wealth

Masked gunmen strike an exclusive sports car.

Police pursuit interceptor Kaitlyn Thorn takes control.

She snaps the cuffs on the driver, gorgeous cocky Randolph Quinn, the world's richest banker. He doesn't make small-talk but he wants to make love.

Sackman-Platinum bank launder the dirty sheets of the underworld. They know where the bodies are buried. As Kaitlyn throws off all sexual chains, she surrenders to pleasure, wealth and intrigue with Randolph.

Police chiefs let her run, encouraging her wild erotic passion for her man and money. In London, Paris, Milan and New York, Kaitlyn exposes herself to a wild trail of evil and greed.

Is everything what it seems?

Could lust, riches and sexual pleasure hide a simple heart in love?

http://www.smarturl.it/webwealth

Power

A thug pulls a knife on a mean London street. Police constable Olivia Johnston-Denny faces him down. A regular day. When irresistible American congressman Jackson T Paine intervenes, her life is changed forever. A spark of attraction starts an inferno of erotic heat.

In a world of bitter political division and deceit, this one man offers straightforward country-style honesty. Tipped as a future president, ruthless opponents plot his downfall, by smear or by death. Olivia and Jackson cannot risk involvement, but forces of emotion and passion run out of control.

A merciless kidnap and gangster style international bankers fill Olivia's working days. Only in the shadows can she express her love for Jackson.

When her professional investigations lead to her lover's door she stands at a dark abyss. Is he everything he seems?

She has to know the truth as a cop and as a woman in love.

http://www.smarturl.it/webpowerhttp://www.smarturl.it/webpower

Sub-Prime (#1 The Love in a Hopeless Place Collection)

Two powerless beings are swept together in a transient struggle for survival. Could the human spirit transcend the brutality and indifference of their brief experience before they are once again swept helplessly apart? Far more than a love story—this is a story about love

Sub-Prime: a short story of our times.

Available as an e-book (For Kindle and Kindle Apps for iPad, Android, PC MAC etc.) at Amazon worldwide:

http://smarturl.it/Sub-Prime

The Chosen (#2 The Love in a Hopeless Place Collection)

A woman, a man, a van, and a plan. When the luck runs out; the lucky walk away. A short story set in the extremis of everyday.

Available as an e-book (For Kindle and Kindle Apps for iPad, Android, PC MAC etc.) at Amazon worldwide on the following link:

https://www.emmacalin.com/ChosenThe

Escape to Love (#3 The Love in a Hopeless Place Collection)

A woman on the run from domestic violence with no one but her vulnerable autistic teenage child as a companion lives in isolation and fear. While her hand-to-mouth scenarios are played out in the shadow of a threatening suspense, a story of crime and love unfolds around her.

Angela (#4 The Love in a Hopeless Place Collection)

A mystery tale of a late-night taxi ride where the final passenger may not be all that she seems.

http://www.smarturl.it/shortAngela

Love in a Hopeless Place (#5 The Love in a Hopeless Place Collection)

A mature woman finds the truth of herself. She cannot go back even though physical and emotional violence erupt around her.

Dare she give in to love?

Will sexual passion and fear overwhelm her stable life?

Whom can she trust to love her for herself?

http://www.smarturl.it/LIAHP

The Love in a Hopeless Place Collection

Emma Calin's complete set of short stories and novelettes, available in one bargain "boxed set." This edition includes *Sub-Prim*e, *The Chosen, Escape To Love, Love In A Hopeless Place* and short story: *Angela.* It is available as a paperback and e-book from Amazon Worldwide.

http://www.smarturl/it/LIAHPCollection

Children's Books by Emma Calin

The "Once Upon a NOW!" Series

The *"Once Upon a NOW!"* books form a series of illustrated, interactive children's stories, in the true fairy tale tradition with modern-day settings. Each is available in paperback, Kindle, and audio book formats. Digital versions come with clickable links to bonus video clips, photos, and drawings to color. The paperback has QR codes to scan and take you to the same bonus material to enrich the stories.

http://smarturl.it/OUANAmazon

Coming soon… The complete Box Set of all three books in the *"Once Upon a Now Series"* for Kindle. Grab this bargain bundle here:

http://www.smarturl.it/OUANBoxed

Alf The Workshop Dog

How could a scruffy dog in a bus depot, and the call of crows link back to another world of power and love? The ancient Kingdom of Zanubia and a stray dog looking for scraps in an inner-city repair garage, hold the secret. A wicked king, a beautiful girl, a young prince and the struggle between right and wrong maintain the fable tradition.

http://www.smarturl.it/Alf

Isabella's Pink Bicycle

There's something strange in the woodshed....

A poor little girl in a faraway land dreams of riding a pink bicycle. When she meets a strange animal, her dreams come true. Her happiness turns to sadness when a tragedy occurs in the town and her father doesn't come home. Maybe her new magic friend can find him?

http://www.smarturl.it/IsabellaPink

Kool Kid Kruncha and the High Trapeze

Charlie finds it tough when his parents divorce, but Auntie Kate helps him overcome his greatest fear.

When Charlie has to move from the country into the city, he leaves behind his home, his mates, and his beloved football team. He will need to make new friends. With his small size and red hair, some people aren't kind to him. He wonders if he can face another day at school.

A trip to the circus gives him the strength to see himself and others in a new way.

http://www.smarturl.it/Kruncha

About Emma Calin

Novelist, philosopher, blogger, poet, would be master chef. A woman pedaling between Peckham & Pigalle, in search of passion & enduring romance.

Emma Calin writes romance novels, gritty short stories and children's fiction about love and survival in the 21st century. She has published a number of digital, paperback, and audio books which are available from Amazon and other good bookstores worldwide.

She blogs about her dual life in St-Savinien sur Charente in Southwest France and Romsey, a market town in southern England. She feels extremely lucky to be able to experience the world and life through these two very different lenses. She spends any time she can, when not writing, on her tandem exploring the countryside.

Emma also records and produces audio books and plays the trombone (although not at the same time).

Find Emma Calin on the Internet:

Website: http://www.emmacalin.com

Blog: http://emmacalinblog.com/

Twitter: http://twitter.com/EmmaCalin

Facebook: http://www.facebook.com/emma.calin

Facebook Fan Page:
http://www.facebook.com/Knockout.Romance.Novel

Goodreads:
http://www.goodreads.com/author/show/4915751.Emma_
Calin

Amazon Author Page:
http://smarturl.it/EmmaAmazonWorldwide

Publisher

This book was published by Gallo-Romano Media. For details of other books and authors or if you would like to submit your book for publishing:

Email: contact@gallo-romano.co.uk

Web: http://www.gallo-romano.com